RUTHLESS TRUTHS

VEILED VENGEANCE BOOK ONE

HEATHER RENEE

HARPER REED

ISBN: 978-19577312 54

Line Editing and Proofing: Jamie from Holmes Edits

Cover: Covers by Aura

Illustrations: Art by Kalynne

CONTENTS

A Note From The Author   v

Chapter 1   1
Chapter 2   11
Chapter 3   23
Chapter 4   35
Chapter 5   43
Chapter 6   49
Chapter 7   61
Chapter 8   73
Chapter 9   85
Chapter 10   93
Chapter 11   103
Chapter 12   111
Chapter 13   123
Chapter 14   135
Chapter 15   143
Chapter 16   157
Chapter 17   165
Chapter 18   175
Chapter 19   181
Chapter 20   193
Chapter 21   201
Chapter 22   213
Chapter 23   221
Chapter 24   233
Chapter 25   241
Chapter 26   253

Chapter 27   261
Chapter 28   269

Stay in Touch   277
Also by the Authors   279
About the Authors   283

A NOTE FROM THE AUTHOR

For my readers that have been following me for a while now...this is nothing like my past works. There is no magic, but there is plenty of murder and angst that eventually leads to some very detailed sex scenes. Keep reading if you're intrigued!

For the reader that's looking for that darker romance escape, I hope you enjoy the first part of Luca and Olivia's story, but be warned...

This does end on a cliffhanger and there are a few triggers including, but not limited to, an assault that could have turned into rape and the emotional trauma that follows—neither done by the love interest—along with some degradation, imprisonment, and as mentioned above, some casual murdering. After all, this is a *mafia* romance :)

So, sit back and enjoy the action in *all* its forms.

XOXO,

Heather Renee

DEDICATION

*To anyone who ever doubted you, made you feel less than,
as if you couldn't, or shouldn't, be perfectly you, or
anything other than fucking awesome...
Let's give them a giant middle finger together and hope
they eat shit. Literally and figuratively.*

1

OLIVIA

Silence is deafening. It's a saying I've heard many times before. Yet, until now, I'd never truly grasped its meaning. I should consider myself lucky for that small fact, but there isn't anything *lucky* about losing the only parent I've ever truly had.

As I sit in the aged living room of my mother's house—the place I called home throughout my childhood—it's only now hitting me that she's gone.

Gone and never coming back.

Though it's been three days since her passing, between the constant flow of visitors and funeral arrangements, I haven't had a moment to fully accept that I'll never see her again.

I'll never smell her floral perfume or rub her pink lipstick off my cheek or need a chiropractor after one of her all-encompassing, exuberant hugs. Worse, the sound of her sweet voice is no longer here to tell me everything is going to be okay.

The unknown of not having my mother available to me, no matter how crazy she could be, terrifies and paralyzes me all at once.

I lose myself in the once vibrant but now faded and peeling yellow wallpaper of the living room, trying my best to hold on to any one emotion, but just as soon as I start to feel anything, it's swallowed by the pain.

Still, regardless of the physical aches consuming me, I don't really cry. Not like I feel I should be. Not the sobbing, chest-opening wails I would have expected.

Silence is deafening, I repeat to myself.

Palpable. Overwhelming. The sole backdrop to the kind of grief that makes me fear every moment of the future that I'll face without her.

I adored my mother. She was an amazing woman who loved me with her whole heart and then some. Who gave more than she ever received, who would want more for me than this excruciating numbness I've found myself trapped in. It feels as if my deeper emotions have abandoned me, leaving me caged inside myself, unable to properly release the agony inside me.

My best friend Tori places her hand on my shoulder, interrupting my dazed state. "Liv?" she asks softly.

Startled, I wipe the tears from my face and look up at her. Her blonde hair is braided over her shoulder and her round cheeks are flushed, making her appear much younger than twenty-nine.

She brushes her hands over her black dress and bites the corner of her mouth. It's a nervous tic she's had since we met in grade school.

"What is it?" I ask, then clear my throat when I don't recognize the monotone cadence of my voice.

"I found some stuff that you're going to want to see," she says. "I wanted to wait since the funeral was today, but it's time sensitive."

She reaches for my hand, and I let her pull me up from the threadbare forest green chair, guiding me toward the third bedroom in the house. The one that has slowly transformed into a cluttered storage space over the years.

It's the one area of the house I've avoided since finding out Mom died. The musty odor and the uncertainty of what I might uncover within its walls have kept me at bay.

Yes, my mother loved me fiercely, but the woman had her secrets. Some I'd sussed out over the years, and others were left concealed. I like to pretend there's good reason for that, but deep down, I've been too afraid of what I might find.

Tori hands me a stack of mail. "These are bills for the house. I know you already put your notice in at your apartment with the intent of living here—" she bites her lip again "—but maybe they'll let you renege on that."

My mouth presses into a hard line, already knowing that's impossible. I lived in a rent-controlled apartment in Portland, Oregon, a city where everything has tripled in price over the last few years. My place was snatched up before the ink even dried on my notice.

"They can't be that bad," I say, taking them from her,

hoping that whatever Mom left in savings will be enough to cover what's owed.

Then, my stomach sinks.

The top envelope reads "Final Notice" in red ink on the front.

Fuck, Mom. What have you done?

I tear it open, even more irritated that she hadn't even cared to read the contents of something so important.

It's a letter from the county. Mom hasn't paid the property taxes on this house in six years.

Six fucking years.

There's an auction date set to sell the house in just two weeks. They sent this over a month ago.

Seriously, Mom. What in the ever-loving fuck?

She never mentioned struggling with the bills. I would have helped her if she had. Though, in reality, I'm not sure what I could have done, considering I could barely make ends meet after paying for my student loans and other living expenses.

Working in accounts receivable at a medical warehouse doesn't exactly bring home hefty paychecks, but I have plans—plans to save up and start my own accounting firm, instead of working under someone else's thumb for the rest of my life.

"That's not all," Tori says, her voice tinged with further concern. "The power is scheduled to be shut off tomorrow, and the water is also on final notice, with most balances due in full."

If my mother was still alive, I'd be tempted to strangle her myself.

God, that's a fucked-up thought, but damn it. This house is all I have left of her and my childhood. Keeping this place for myself was always the plan. Now, I have no idea what I'm going to do.

"I can't afford all this," I admit, frustration building inside me. At least I'm not numb any longer. "The stupid thing is she has money in savings. She could have paid some of these bills months ago."

A crease forms between Tori's brows. "Do you think she knew she was..."

"Going to die from that blood clot?" I finish the sentence Tori is too sweet to say so bluntly. "Hell, I don't know. My mother was a lot of things, but that seems a little farfetched."

Then again, while all my friends were showered with love and sheltered from the harsh realities of the world, my mom and I were abandoned by my father. He left us when I was nine, with no notice or even a reason, according to Mom. That frustration forced me to grow up before I even had a driver's license, and Mom learned to wear a lot of hats she shouldn't have had to. Yet, being a psychic was never one of them. She couldn't have known she was going to die. Not like that.

Thinking back to my childhood, I'm once again reminded of how angry I've been with my absent father over the years. He turned his back on us and never once looked back or wrote a letter. Searching this room is the only way I might find answers, but that adds to my dread. I think this is one thing better left in the past.

Mom and I did what we had to do to take care of each

other, and we survived—until now. Nothing else matters. Well, except finding a way to make sure I don't lose this house.

"How much is in savings?" Tori asks, bringing me back to the present conversation. "Maybe you can explain the situation, arrange payment plans, and buy yourself more time to decide what you're going to do."

This is why I love Tori. She's my polar opposite. She believes in all the good in the world and the power of positivity.

Except her normal good juju vibes aren't going to save me now. I need cold hard cash.

"I don't know. Most of these say final notice, due in full," I answer with a sigh, skimming some of the papers she's already laid out. "I'll figure it out. Why don't you go home to Greg?"

She shakes her head. "He knows you need me. I'm not leaving you like this."

I grab her shoulders and gently force her out of the hellish room. "Go home, Tori. I haven't had a moment to myself in days. Let me process all of this, and I'll catch you up tomorrow on whatever I come up with."

"Are you sure?" she asks, still trying to resist my movements as I guide her to the front door.

"Absolutely," I assure her. "I've got this."

I use the three words I know will make her smile and it works like a charm. Her arms wrap around me in a tight embrace. "Yes, you do. Everything is going to be fine. If you have to come stay with me and Greg for a while, then you can do that, too."

There isn't a chance in hell of that happening, but it's sweet of her to offer. I can't stand her boyfriend, but Tori doesn't know that. He makes her happy, and she loves him. I wouldn't ever taint that for her, even if something about his domineering personality grates on my nerves.

Not when she's pretty much the only person left in this world that I can't live without.

———

It's midnight, and instead of staying at the house to figure out a solution to my problems, I find myself at the bar with my co-worker Sandi. We're not close friends like I am with Tori, but I enjoy Sandi's company and the way she's capable of making me forget my problems. At least most days. Today might not be one of those.

Sandi's a brunette bombshell in her forties who kicks ass at work and is sexy as fuck on a stripper pole. Though, she doesn't take her clothes off. It's just a hobby that I'm slightly envious of but haven't had the vagina to try myself.

As she slams her shot glass on the counter, a mischievous grin spreads across her oval face. "I have an idea. A great fucking idea."

My brow arches, curiosity piqued. "Do tell."

Earlier, when Sandi called me, I briefly mentioned my predicament, and she insisted that my sorry ass needed a drink. I couldn't argue with her, and now, five drinks in, I have to admit she was right. The alcohol has temporarily whisked me away from the abyss of despair that consumed me earlier, a place I desperately hope to avoid returning to.

Even though we've never been overly close, more co-workers than friends, her strong personality is something I'm currently clinging to.

"My aunt owns an art gallery," she starts. "Every year they hold an annual charity fundraiser—"

I cut her off. "I'm not okay with handouts when I know there are people in much worse positions than I am who could use the help."

She shakes her head. "Shut up and let me talk."

Yep. I needed her tonight.

Sandi continues. "So, this fundraiser. They go all out to draw in a crowd, and this year, it's about winning dates."

My eyes widen, and I swallow hard. "Like prostitutes?"

She shoves playfully at my thigh and shakes her head. "Jesus, Olivia. No. It's purely platonic and just for fun and charity. My aunt has me signed up, but you could take my place and—"

I interrupt her again. "Umm, what about Malcolm? I thought you were happily married."

She finishes her last shot and laughs, her hazel eyes twinkling under the neon bar lights. "Like I said. Fun and charity. Even Mal is up on the auction block. It's not a real date. Just something to entice in the older crowd with money. Hell, according to my aunt, some of them never even happen. Bidders are either stuck-up socialites flaunting their deep pockets or lonely widows looking for someone to chat with while supporting a good cause."

"Okay," I say, drawing out the word. "I'm still confused on how me taking your place could help with all my newly acquired bills."

"Well," she says with a smack of her lips. "Each volunteer receives a small payment as a token of gratitude for being ogled at. I was going to donate mine to the children's hospital that they're raising the funds for, but right now, you need it more than they do."

"And I don't have to sleep with anyone?" I ask, because this sounds too good to be true.

"Nope," she replies confidently. "I promise. You just need to agree now, because it's happening in two days."

When I hesitate, she continues, "Seriously. I'll make one phone call and you can take my place. And, if you manage to snag the highest bid of the night, which you can absolutely do, you'll bring home fifteen hundred bucks."

With the three grand still left in my mom's account, the money I've been saving up, and this opportunity, there might be a chance to appease the county and halt the auction. Surely, they'd have some sympathy for me, given the circumstances...

Or they just might laugh in my face, and I would have put myself on display for nothing. My stomach churns as I drum my nails on the bar top. I'm not sure I can do this. Any other day, it might sound fun, but I know what's at stake if I can't get this money. The pressure has me hesitating.

I reach for my fruity cocktail and down the last of it, letting the remnants of alcohol burn down my throat as I do my best to let go of all the things that I can't change. At least for the moment.

The glass touches down on the counter a little harder than I intend, and I stare at it while it teeters briefly before balancing back out and staying upright.

Fuck it. I don't want to live with regret if I run short of money and have to remember the moment I told Sandi no.

"I'll do it," I declare with feigned bravado. "But you'll have to help with my hair, makeup, and picking out a dress."

Sandi places a hand over her chest and swoons. "Oh, girl. I've got you. We're going to have so much fun with this, and you're going to be the star of the night."

I'm not entirely sure how I feel about being the center of attention, but if it means earning the cash I desperately need without compromising myself, then why the hell not?

Plus, as long as I sleep until noon tomorrow, I can't regret this in the morning.

2

OLIVIA

There are maybe ten minutes left before I'm going to be "auctioned off." Sandi has already left me to go take her seat in the crowd, and despite her repeated assurances that this isn't the first step to becoming a hooker, I'm still unsure about my decision to be here tonight.

Maybe it's the waiting crowd or the worry of not being bid on at all, but *something* has my chest constricting and lungs working overtime. I just hope I don't find out what that is.

Casting one final glance in the mirror, I admire my sleek, straight hair. The ebony strands cascade flawlessly around my face, accentuating my fair skin. My makeup is done heavier than I normally like, but with the highest bid bonus on the line, I hadn't asked Sandi to hold back.

Shimmering eyeshadow and black eyeliner make my bright blue eyes look even more vibrant than normal. My lips are plumped with light red lipstick, while an unnatural blush stains my cheeks. The black sequin dress clings to my curves, it's deep V-neckline showcasing my breasts, but not enough that I feel overly exposed.

The hemline hits midthigh and, as I stand there in three-inch heels, my legs feel longer than ever, even though I stand only a few inches above five feet. My hands slide over the fabric of the dress one last time before a gentle knock sounds at the door of the dressing room.

A friendly, older redhead woman peeks her head inside. "We're ready for you, sweetheart."

I nod silently and follow her toward the stage that's been set up in the third-floor banquet hall at one of Portland's finest hotels. I caught a brief glimpse of it earlier when we arrived, but nothing could have prepared me for the onslaught of blinding lights that I'm hit with as soon as I'm nudged past the curtain.

"And last but certainly not least, we have Olivia Danes," the speaker's voice booms with enthusiasm. "Ms. Danes, a lifelong resident of our great town, is a college graduate with a degree in accounting and business."

Do not throw up. Do not throw up. Do. Not. Throw. Up.

I repeat the chant inside my head with every step I take down the short runway. A smile is forced to my face as I desperately try to find Sandi in the crowd to give myself a focal point, but with all the fucking lights, everything beyond the first couple rows is a blur.

"She enjoys cozy movie nights at home and relaxing weekends at the beach," the speaker continues, providing a description of myself that I hadn't penned. Sandi must have, and I kind of hate her right now.

"Olivia was a gymnast when she was young, but now, she finds solace in starting her days with a bit of yoga," he says, and as I turn away from the audience to walk back toward the speaker, I'm certain my face is ten shades of red.

Not because I'm embarrassed about the likelihood of all these men now thinking about my "flexibility," but because I'm ready to strangle my co-worker. Okay, maybe both.

"Now, let's start the bidding off at one-thousand dollars," the silver fox speaker says, adjusting his bowtie as I reach his side.

As soon as the bidding starts, I'm frozen in place, doing my best to "smile pretty" as Sandi instructed before leaving me earlier. The weight of knowing I'm doing this in a desperate attempt to save the link I have to my mother continues to press in on me. I know one day I won't ache from this loss as I do now, but if I lose her house, too, even if it's not my fault, I'm not sure I could bear the devastation.

The speaker places his hand on my shoulders, disrupting the thoughts plaguing my consciousness. The buzzing in my ears eases, and I only catch the last part of what he says.

"...and we have our new record for the evening, ladies and gentlemen!"

What in the actual fuck?

Who are these people, and why do they have so much

money to blow on a date that, according to Sandi, will possibly never even happen?

An older gentleman stands in the front row. From where I'm standing, I can make out his stout frame and potbelly. "Twenty-five thousand dollars!" he shouts, raising a white paddle in the air with the number eighty-seven on it.

Seriously, this is insane.

Another man sitting only a row behind the recent bidder doesn't stand like the balding man, but his intense gaze locks on me and he casually raises his paddle. Where are stupid lights when I *want* them to blind me?

I freeze for a beat from the intensity of his dark amber eyes, but that doesn't stop me from taking in the rest of Mr. Tall, Dark, and Sinful.

Strands of umber hair fall over his forehead, but the sides are kept neatly trimmed. His sharp jawline is cleanly shaven, but something tells me he'd look ten times sexier with a bit of stubble. He's wearing a charcoal three-piece suit that I'm certain is tailor-made for him, emphasizing the width of his shoulders.

His tongue peeks out, wetting his lips before he speaks. "Thirty-thousand dollars."

Whereas the old, balding man had shouted, this other, far more delicious specimen, keeps his tone even, and I swear I can still feel his words echoing in my ears.

Fuck me.

I cross my fingers behind my back, silently praying Potbelly doesn't bid again. Seconds of tension tick by before the speaker finally says, "Thirty thousand to Mr. Monroe. Wow, thank you so much everyone…"

I don't hear the rest of what he says. Now that the bidding is done, I follow my previously given instructions and make my way off the stage.

My face still feels flushed from the brief encounter with…*Mr. Monroe*, but I'm still eager to get home. Someone like him won't be claiming a date with the likes of me. A woman who can't even pay her bills without selling herself out.

Back in the dressing room, I change into jeans and a sweatshirt. It might be June, but Oregon nights are always crisp, no matter the time of year.

With all my stuff packed into my oversized purse, I sling the strap over my shoulder and exit the room. The hallways are already packed with people also trying to leave, making it loud as fuck in the small space.

With the nerves caused by being up on that stage still making my head feel off, I decide to find an alternate exit and turn left toward the other side of the hotel. Numerous staff members dressed in white collared shirts and black slacks pass by, but none of them stop me. After what feels like twenty minutes, I finally discover a stairwell that will take me back to the ground floor.

Three flights of stairs later, I end up in front of two doors. One leads to the lobby and the other to the back of the hotel. It'll be a longer walk to where I've parked if I go out the back, but there will be less people.

A longer walk never killed anyone.

I reach into my pocket for my phone while I open the

door, not exactly paying attention to my surroundings. Though, I let out a sigh as the cool, refreshing night air hits my skin. I allow myself a brief moment to relax, closing my eyes as I lean against the door frame.

My phone vibrates in my hand, but I also hear the scuffle of shoes ahead of me that has me finally glancing out in front of me to confirm that I'm not alone. Too many men to count stand there staring at me, many of them armed with guns, several of which are pointed at me.

Panicking, I reach back for the door to escape inside, but there's no fucking handle. It's an exit only.

I search for...I have no fucking clue, but my situation only gets worse. Between all those men, lying face-up on the asphalt, is someone I recognize from his frequent appearances on the news. Gone is his normally jovial smile, replaced by wide eyes and a bullet hole in his forehead.

Holy fucking shit.

Senator McAdams. He's fucking dead.

A scream catches in my throat as I manage to tear my eyes away from the motionless form, but that doesn't better my situation.

"Kill her," someone demands, and I drop to the ground like a sack of rocks, rolling behind a dumpster as bullets start to fly, the bangs of gunpowder echoing in the small space.

I'm pretty sure I'm screaming, but my pounding heart drowns out the sound. I cover my head with my hands, unaware of what's happening around me as I begin to curl into a tight ball with the hopes of becoming a smaller target that's less likely to be hit with a bullet if anyone comes to find me in the shadows.

My limbs start to go numb, making the decision to run out of the question, even when I hear the gunfire cease. Shouts are shared between men, and another thud sounds from further away. Fuck my life. Bodies are literally dropping all around me.

"Get in the fucking car," a grumbly voice says from much too close and steals my breath.

I have no clue if he's talking to me, but I'm just going to play dead, because there's no possible way I can budge from the ground.

"Are you shot?" he demands, but I still don't answer, partially because I'm so wound up that I'm not even sure I know the answer to his question.

Warm hands force my body to unravel, and I start to fight back, but the snarl that sounds from the darkness shrouding this man has me paralyzed in fear at least for a few seconds.

"You're fine. Now, up."

I'm so fucking far from fine it's almost funny.

When I don't move, he snarls once more, then roughly picks me up, slipping warm hands under my body, their touch bringing an unexpected relief to my cold bones. Until I realize I have no idea who wanted me dead and who is now holding me.

Instinctively, my arm pulls back, and I blindly throw a punch, connecting with something hard, yet clothed.

"Fuck," the same gruff voice says. "I'm trying to fucking save you."

Since it takes my brain more than a second to register what he's said, I hit him once more, but he manages to restrain my wrists with one hand. The growl that comes from deep in his chest finally has me pausing.

At least he's not shooting at me, I think as I stop fighting for the moment until I open my eyes again and see several more dead bodies in the dark alleyway.

"Let me go!" I screech and try to punch my unknown captor again, but he keeps a tight hold on me, locking his arms tightly around me.

He doesn't reply to my demand with words. Instead, the door to an SUV is opened and I'm tossed into the back seat like a damn shopping bag.

I don't bother trying to reason with words. My fingers grasp the latch of the other door and yank hard, hoping to jump out the opposite side, but the fucker won't budge.

"I told you the child locks would come in handy, boss," the driver up front says.

The man who picked me up gets in with his head down, but I still get a good enough look at his face.

"You." I gasp.

He turns toward me, those same piercing amber eyes seeming to penetrate my soul. "I just saved your life. Maybe you should be thanking me instead of glaring."

"But that was Senator McAdams," I say, barely keeping a frightened stutter out of my words. "And you were just in the hotel. How did…"

I don't even know how to finish my question. Too much fucking shit is happening right now.

Someone grabs my neck tightly from the back seat. "Want me to shut her up?"

Mr.... Shit, what last name did the speaker use? My head is too flustered to remember. Either way, the guy who bid on me and just possibly saved my life lifts his lip into a sinister snarl. "Don't fucking touch her."

I try the window this time, but it doesn't open either.

"You're safe, Olivia," he says, softer than any of his previous words but still not kind.

I scoff and cross my arms. "I don't even know who you are, so why should I believe you after what I just saw?"

"I'm Luca Monroe," he says, then looks toward the driver as if his name is the only explanation I need. "Take us to Roe."

Golden eyes glance back at him from the rearview mirror. "Are you sure..."

Luca's hands are clenched into fists. "Do I ever speak without thinking, Jaxon?"

His voice is calm, but I'm certain I'm no safer now than I was when I walked into the alleyway.

Why couldn't I have just braved the crowds? *Why?*

Jaxon doesn't reply, which seems like the safest option for those of us in the vehicle. I scoot further away from Luca, pressing my shoulder into the unyielding window.

Luca pulls out his phone, but I don't even try to sneak

a peek at the screen. Though, it reminds me of the stuff I dropped during the...commotion.

"Stop," I demand.

Jaxon, of course, doesn't listen to me and continues backing out of the alleyway.

"I need my purse," I say to nobody in particular.

"You can buy new stuff," Luca says without looking up from his phone.

Shit. I want to punch his sexy mouth.

"Not everyone is a rich fuck like you," I blurt without thinking, forgetting for a moment about my precarious situation.

His gaze slowly lifts, and once again, his eyes feel as if they burn right through me. "Rich fuck?"

I'm in it now, so I merely shrug. Boldness isn't quite the survival skill I thought I would land on, but here we are. Somehow it seems to be working for me.

"I think that's the first time anyone has called me that." The way he says the words, it's almost as if I've amused him.

"Well, then maybe you need new friends that don't kiss your ass," I add when his attention goes back to his phone.

There's a little voice in my head telling me to shut my fucking mouth and just maybe I'll get out of this... situation alive. Yet, at the same time, I can't override the knee-jerk reaction to show him he doesn't scare me, even though I'm fucking terrified. I mean, he would have let me die back there if he was going to kill me, right? I feel decently confident about that. Or maybe that's just idiocy. I'll find out soon enough.

The SUV fills with silence as we pull onto the main road. Streetlights stream through the windows and into the SUV, and I glance behind me, remembering someone had grabbed my neck. There are two men in the rear seat, one with a wounded shoulder.

"Shit, you're bleeding," I say, surprised by the lack of reaction from anyone else in the vehicle. "Who the fuck are you people?"

The one not wounded leans forward but keeps his hands to himself. He has a scar down his left cheek, dark eyes, a shaved head, and tattoos covering his neck that disappear beneath his black shirt.

"We're nobody," he replies with a smirk that sends a chill down my spine.

Dread instantly fills me. "Nobody" seems a hell of a lot worse than something like a twisted rich people gang. Because if there isn't anyone that knows who these guys really are, how the hell am I going to stand a chance of escaping from them?

3

LUCA

I've attended that fundraiser five years in a row. Each time, I've bid on the final auction of the night, and when I send in my donation, it's always three times what I bid. A little good to balance out the bad.

But this time...I let a pretty face distract me, nearly allowing me to be outbid.

I convinced myself that it didn't matter because I wasn't ever going to see her again, but twenty minutes later, there she is. Walking out of the hotel at the worst possible moment.

A group of Titan Moretti's men had cornered the senator who was smart enough to send a text to me while I assume they were "chatting." But by the time I showed up, McAdams was already dead, and before I could question them about why a man that I frequently used to get things I wanted had a bullet in his head, out walked Olivia.

While another politician can always be bought, I've put myself into a position that I can't easily back out of. I saved a woman I had no business saving. She is nothing to me. Merely a pretty face. Yet, twice now, I've looked into her bright blue eyes and been unable to ignore the twinge in my chest. But it's one I can never admit exists out loud and need to force out of my system.

Her innocence up on that stage, the way she shrunk in on herself, and the surprise on her face that anyone would place a bid that high for her... All of that combined with the fear-filled scream that ripped from her lungs when she saw the senator, I knew I couldn't let her die. She didn't deserve that fate. At least, not today.

Then, there's the feigned strength in her words, the snark she seems to babble with. I don't know why I find it endearing, but fuck, it is.

All that combined makes Olivia Danes a problem. A big fucking problem.

I've killed enough times in my thirty-nine years that I can't remember the body count, and the number of people I've seen die by another's hand would be absurd to most. And it's not like innocents haven't been taken out along the way. Yet, this time, there was no allowing this woman to be harmed. When Moretti's guy ordered Olivia to be killed, I couldn't let it happen.

We'd fired back against them, saving her life, but now there would be retaliation.

All because of a fucking woman I know nothing about.

What the fuck was I thinking?

She's a liability.

Regardless of my reasons for initially saving her, I need to remember that. Worse, I know I should kill her, because letting her go after what she witnessed isn't possible. She could dismantle everything my family has built over the past seven decades, blaming me for that bloodbath in the alleyway. And still, I ignore logic.

A text pops up at the top of my screen.

Titan: It seems we have a problem. You killed my men.

Me: You killed my senator. Without my permission.

Titan: He said he wasn't yours. Maybe I did you a favor. Still, you owe me for my men, and the woman you let live is another problem.

Titan Moretti and I have never been friends, but we've always had a mutual understanding about how we run our businesses. He focuses on drugs and other illicit shit I prefer not to know about, and I keep my hands a little cleaner with other ventures like stock fraud and guns.

Neither of us is a saint. I just prefer for others to believe I am, unlike Moretti. He seems to prefer working in the shadows, very rarely showing his face.

Whenever our business dealings have crossed paths in the past, we've always been able to work something out, but now? I glance over at Olivia and how she's pressed tightly against the door, still attempting to pull on that fucking handle as if it's magically unlocked in the last few minutes.

Her body is covered by jeans and a sweatshirt now, but I have no problem recalling the black dress she'd been wearing on stage, the image etched like a vivid painting in my mind.

The way the sequined fabric hugged her hips, accentuating her feminine allure, sent a primal urge coursing through me. I couldn't help but imagine burying my face between those perfectly sculpted breasts and feeling their softness against my skin. Her legs, toned and shapely, begged to be entwined with mine.

And the contrast of her jet-black hair cascaded down her back like a raven's wing, standing out starkly against her fair skin. But it wasn't just her physical beauty that captivated me. Those piercing blue eyes, as bright as a cloudless day, hold a depth and purity within them that intrigues me beyond words.

She glances up, catching my stare, and for a moment, I see a flicker of defiance in her gaze. It both frustrates and entices me, igniting a fire in my chest that I'm not accustomed to feeling. The clash of emotions intensifies, drawing me deeper into the web she's inadvertently and unknowingly spun around me.

No. This time, I don't think Moretti and I are going to see eye-to-eye.

Me: I'm handling her.

Titan: Unless I see a picture of her being thrown into the Columbia River, I don't think your version of handling it works for me.

Yeah, I didn't think it would.

Me: I'll be in touch.

I won't be. That's a lie to keep him off my back while I figure out what I want to do about this woman.

She's fucking terrified, yet there's a fire in her eyes that tells me that no matter how much fear is pulsing through her veins right now, she's also prepared to claw my eyes out if given the opportunity.

What's worse is that for some fucked-up reason, it makes me want to bend her over my bed and fuck the fire right out of her. A twisted desire to break her over and over again until she no longer recognizes herself in the mirror. Until I'm no longer trapped in whatever spell she's weaving.

We pull into the Roe compound. It's an old apartment building that has been turned into the private living quarters for myself and a select few I trust most. It's also good for conducting business that needs to remain private.

Like hiding a woman who's seen more than she should have.

As the car stops in my designated parking spot near the elevator, Jaxon steps out, ready to open my door. However, I interrupt him by rolling down the window, moving my gaze back to Olivia. "Everybody go the fuck away," I command, my voice leaving no room for argument. "Except you."

I keep my eyes on her shaking form as I roll the window up and wait for Damon and Vin to go out the back hatch.

Jaxon watches me through the tinted window. I can tell he doesn't agree with the choice I've made tonight, but too fucking bad. He's not the boss. I am. I'll run my business however I see fit.

Once the three of them have entered the elevator, I unbuckle my seatbelt, then lock my stare on Olivia's rather defiant one. "What you saw tonight—"

"I didn't see anything," she interrupts, her voice laced with bravado I'm not believing. "Just let me go."

A grin tugs at the corners of my mouth, and I watch how she swallows nervously, staring at my smile. "You see, in my line of work, things don't work that way. We don't just *let*—"

"What kind of business are you in, Mr. Monroe?" she interjects, her tone dripping with snark.

A surge of irritation courses through me, my hands itching with the desire to assert dominance, to teach her a lesson. But I choose a different approach. I decide to inject a little more fear into her veins.

Reaching across the car, I wrap my fingers around her throat, applying just enough pressure to feel every hitch of her breath beneath my touch.

"Don't interrupt me," I state calmly, yet with an underlying threat I'm certain she doesn't miss. "You should have died back there, but thanks to me, you're still alive. For now. So, it would be in your best interest *not* to piss me off."

I pause, observing the widening of her light blue eyes, now glossed over with trepidation. "Good," I say. "We're going to walk into my building, and you're not going to be difficult. Do I make myself clear?"

She nods again, but since I don't trust her compliance, I add, "I may have spared your life, but I have no qualms about tying you up and throwing you in a cell. Feel free to tempt me if you'd like to find out what that's like."

I release her and open my door, but she hesitates, not following my lead. I turn back to her. "Does that idea of a cell sound appealing?" I ask with a tilt of my head.

She shrugs, her nonchalance fueling my frustration. "I mean, if it keeps me from getting killed or choked..."

Clearly, she's still not properly scared.

"Get the fuck out the car, Olivia," I demand, growling with authority.

She lets out an actual fucking sigh, blatantly insulting me, then slides across the bench seat. "You could say please."

Once she's standing beside the SUV, I slam the door shut, narrowly miss hitting her shoulder, and use my other hand to push her against the cool metal. "I don't fucking say please. If you think any of this is a joke, I'll quickly show you otherwise."

She blinks, but wisely chooses to remain silent. I grab

her arm firmly and drag her toward the elevator. She's going in the fucking cell, whether she likes it or not.

It doesn't matter that her defiance makes my dick awaken unlike it has in much too long. I won't tolerate disobedience. Not from anyone.

I press the button for the sublevels, leaving it there long enough for my thumbprint to be scanned and access to be given. This is where the darkest and most illicit aspects of our business occur. A place deep underground, encased in brick and virtually soundproof.

Maybe with her out of my sight, I'll be able to figure out what the fuck I'm going to do with her in a more permanent capacity.

Keep her, a voice inside my head suggests, but I scoff at the idea.

As appealing as that could be, Olivia doesn't strike me as the type of woman who can be *kept,* and I won't allow her to be a distraction to the life I've painstakingly constructed.

During the elevator ride, Olivia remains silent, but I don't release my tight grip on her bicep. As the doors open, I step out, pulling her along with me.

The putrid stench of death permeates the air, and I sense her slight stiffening. "Where are you taking me?" she asks, her voice laced with anxiety.

"To your temporary room," I reply with a mixture of authority and veiled promise. "Once you decide to be more compliant, your accommodations *might* improve. It's up to you."

"What the fuck does that mean?" she snaps and I tsk, shaking my head.

"I suppose you'll just have to find out." I open the steel door to the first cell, one I know doesn't get used as often as the others and should be...relatively clean. "There's a blanket somewhere in there and a bucket. Use them however you see fit."

I shove her inside, slamming the door closed and plunging her into darkness. A wicked grin spreads across my face as I relish in the sound of her hurling curses and insults in my direction.

"You son of a bitch! You can't fucking do this!" she screeches, her cries echoing through the hallway as I step away, heading back toward the stairs.

At the last second, I briefly turn back and lift the opening where food can be slid through if we choose to. "I already have," I respond, then drop the flap and walk toward the stairs that lead back to the main levels of the house, deliberately making my steps heavier to ensure Olivia hears my departure.

Her shouts and empty threats trail after me until the elevator doors close, cutting off the sounds, and I head upstairs. Once I'm on the first floor, I proceed toward my office, confident that Jaxon is waiting for me.

He might follow my orders, but that doesn't always mean he does so without question. It frequently frustrates me, but I'm not too proud or stubborn to understand his value. Most importantly, and likely because he's my oldest friend, Jaxon typically only questions me in private, helping to ensure that he'll avoid a bullet in the back of his skull.

Sure enough, when I enter my office with its industrial style décor—red brick walls, remnants from the original construction—I find Jaxon standing in front of the metal and wood shelves lining the right wall. His hands are tucked into the pockets of his black slacks, and there is blood splatter on the sleeve of his white dress shirt.

"Where is she?" he asks, turning around to face me.

I make my way to the desk, crafted from the same wood and metal as the shelves. "In the first cell downstairs."

As I move the mouse, my computer awakens. I want to check if Olivia is still raging or if she's finally succumbed to the reality of her situation.

Jaxon takes a seat in one of the black leather chairs in front of my desk and raises an eyebrow at me. "I thought you might tie her to your bed, judging by the way you were looking at her all evening."

"The thought crossed my mind," I admit with a smirk, "but then I would have to gag her, and I'd much rather have her mouth occupied with other things." A few clicks, and a night vision image of Olivia appears on the screen. She's still standing by the cell door, arms crossed, but surprisingly not screaming her lungs out.

"Luca," Jaxon warns, his tone tinged with concern. "I can handle her if you don't want to."

My gaze hardens, and I meet his eyes swiftly. "No."

"But there's no way this can end well."

I know he's trying to make me see reason, but there isn't a part of me that gives a single fuck.

"I don't care," I retort firmly. "Nobody touches her but me."

Jaxon's gaze drops to my desk, his reluctant submission evident. "Let me know if you change your mind."

I won't, but there's no need to tell him that. I'm done with this conversation. My attention returns to the live feed of Olivia where I can see a night vision version of her on the screen. Her raven hair shields most of her face from view, but it doesn't block the rapid rise and fall of chest, indicating her lingering fury.

Perhaps she's saving her energy for when I later return. The thought gives me one too many images that I don't need in my mind.

"What do you want me to do about Titan?" Jaxon asks, standing at the door longer than I expect.

I turn off the screen, no longer desiring the distraction that Olivia represents. My hands rest on my lap as I lean back in my chair. "Let's keep an eye on their crew for the next week while we wait to see who gets blamed for the senator's death. I don't want to act rashly."

"Such as bringing the eyewitness home?" he mutters under his breath.

My fist slams down on the desk, causing everything atop it to tremble. "No more, Jaxon. I'm well aware you disagree with my decision tonight, but it's done, and what I choose to do with the woman is not up for debate. Is that clear?"

He knocks lightly on the doorframe. "Crystal. I'll be around if you need me."

I watch him leave, and once the door is closed behind him, I release a heavy breath, running both hands over my face in an unsuccessful attempt to quell the frustration building within me.

What the fuck am I going to do with Olivia Danes?

4

OLIVIA

The walls of the cell close in on me, their cold touch seeping into my bones. I'm still reeling from my own audacity, the way I defied Luca and landed myself in this miserable cage. Fear, raw and pulsing, courses through my veins, making me someone I'm not. Sure, I can banter with the best of them, but being defiant to someone who likely wouldn't blink twice at murdering me? Not something I expected of myself.

With Luca gone, and me alone in the darkness of this cage, all that remains is a shell of uncertainty and vulnerability.

I press my hands against the metal door, feeling the chill against my palms. How did I end up here? How did I get entangled with a man like Luca Monroe when just hours ago I was standing on a stage for charity?

The minutes tick by, and even though the room is nearly black inside, I stay close to the concrete walls, sliding my palm over its rough edges until my boots kick the blanket that Luca mentioned.

Do I deserve so much fucking better than a single scrap of fabric? Absolutely. But the longer I'm in here, the more adrenaline that leaves me, the colder I get, and it's time to give in to my circumstances.

I won't win against Luca. Not with defiance. He made that clear.

There had been a moment in the SUV when I'd thought he was going to devour every inch of my body, and hell, if that hadn't made my own pulse increase with the thrill that thought elicited. A stupidity on my part that I don't understand and hope to keep at bay.

Yet, minutes later, he threw me into this damn cage like an animal.

The wool from the blanket itches my hands and neck, and though I can't see my breath, I'm certain it's coming out in white puffs from the low temperature of the room.

I blink several times in hopes that I'll be able to see something, but the darkness doesn't change. Realizing I'm not going anywhere soon, I press my back against the wall, thankful as fuck that I'd changed back into my black boots, jeans, and my favorite Multnomah Falls sweatshirt.

I pull the hood up and lean my head into the corner before closing my eyes. My chest burns from the gamut of emotions, but I force my mind to settle, counting back from one-hundred and starting over until the horror of my predicament dissipates and weariness pulls me under.

Only it doesn't last.

What feels like seconds later, a loud bang sounds

from the hallway, and I'm back on my feet before I can take a full breath.

The sound of footsteps echoes through the corridor outside the cell, and my heart jumps into my throat. Is it *him*? Is he coming back? The anticipation tightens my chest, and my hands shake, waiting for the inevitable.

Sure enough, the door swings open, and there he stands, like a specter of darkness against the flickering light above his head. Luca's piercing cognac eyes lock onto me, his gaze a storm of intensity. A mixture of annoyance and curiosity dances across his features, and I can't help but feel exposed under his scrutiny.

"Have you had enough time to reflect on your actions?" he asks, his voice steady and commanding, while also oddly soothing to my frayed nerves.

I'm tempted to tell him to fuck off. No clue why this is my innate reaction around a murderer, and it takes solid effort to rein in the temper I don't normally have. "Considering you left me in the dark, I'm not sure how much time has passed, but I'm sure it's been long enough."

So, my temper has been quelled, but clearly not the snark. Hopefully I can make this work, but I'm starting to see that I must have missed "death wish" on my bingo card for the month.

He stands so still, he might as well be a statue. Hell, I'm not even sure he's breathing, but that doesn't mean I don't see *him*. The way the shadows fall beneath the sharp lines of his jaw, emphasizing the strong angles of his face. As if darkness itself has claimed him, a manifestation of his brooding nature.

I also notice the changes in his appearance since our last encounter. He's discarded his tie, vest, and suit coat, no longer confined by the trappings of formality. Instead, he stands before me in black slacks and a crisp white dress shirt. The sleeves are rolled up, revealing the taut muscles of his forearms.

Involuntarily, I lick my lips and take in a deep breath.

Fuck, I'm in so much trouble—and such an idiot.

The silence is palpable, broken only by the distant hum of electricity running through the hidden wires of this mysterious place. It's almost as if I can feel their vibrations, a subtle reminder of the unseen dangers lurking in the corners. The air is heavy with anticipation, charged with an energy I can't quite comprehend. Or more likely, don't want to.

His heavy stare is still locked on me, and my body shivers. I want to blame it on the coldness still pressing in around me, but I know that's a lie.

"Oh, Raven," he titters. "I was wrong about you."

"My name is Olivia," I correct, but my voice isn't as strong as it was moments before.

The brief smirk that lifts from his lips tells me he's fully aware of what my name is and probably more than I'm okay with him knowing about me.

"Let me remind you of your situation," he says with a calm that infuriates me, because I'm nothing of the sort in his presence.

"You fucked up walking into that alley," he

continues. "You saw things you weren't supposed to, and now that makes you a liability, not only to me, but to the other men that were there."

My throat bobs, understanding that "liabilities" aren't usually a good thing to men like him.

"But I did pay for your company, and I do hate to waste my money," he adds, not making me feel better in the slightest.

"You're going to keep me prisoner all because you had the winning bid in that auction?" I manage to voice my question, the words laden with disbelief. The very notion of continuing to be confined in this claustrophobic cell sends another wave of unease crashing over me.

His head tilts forward, the glint in his stare intensifying, and a chill runs down my spine. "That's up to you," he replies, his voice dripping with calculated detachment. "I'll give you the option of earning your freedom. Given you stopped screaming, tonight you've earned a mattress."

A flicker of hope sparks within me, albeit fragile. A bed, a semblance of comfort amidst the captivity. It's a small reprieve, a gesture that hints at the possibility of escape. But his words also carry an unspoken threat, a reminder that he holds the power to decide my fate. My gaze follows his movements as he steps back, effortlessly pulling a single bed from the hallway and tossing it into the room.

The mattress lands with a dull thud, a stark contrast to the heavy weight pressing against my chest. It's a tangible side effect to my current situation, an imprisonment that extends beyond physical confines. "Let's see how you do tomorrow before we talk about what comes next," he adds, his voice laced with a sense of foreboding.

"You can't do this," I whisper, my voice barely audible, even to my own ears. Desperation is beginning to take over, mingling with the fear that clenches at my heart and taking away all the bravado I previously summoned.

With three steady strides, he closes the distance between us, his hand shooting out to grab at my throat once again. The touch is domineering, with an almost soothing firmness, considering he isn't actually choking me. It's a calculated act, assumingly meant to instill fear without causing harm. The thought forces me to feel the weight of his control, his power over me, and it only adds to the confusion swirling within.

"Oh, I can and I will, Little Raven," he retorts, his voice dripping with a dangerous mix of amusement and something far more sinister. The cell seems to shrink, the walls closing in around me, as if to suffocate any last shred of hope I've been clinging to. The bitter tang of tension lingers in the air, stealing every breath I take.

"Why?" My voice trembles with a mix of curiosity and desperation. "Why not just kill me and be done with it?"

I hold my breath, waiting for his response, dreading the truth that may lie within his words. Life may have seemed bleak this past week, ever since the gut-wrenching loss of my mother, but I am far from ready to embrace death or a lifetime of torment.

His grip on my throat loosens slightly, his fingers grazing my skin as he releases me. His stare intensifies, a storm brewing in his eyes, and I brace myself for his answer. "Because, Little Raven," he begins, his voice a low, dangerous whisper, "your suffering brings me more satisfaction than mere death ever could."

The revelation hangs in the air, a chilling truth that pierces through my defenses. My heart pounds in my chest, the weight of my predicament settling over me like a leaden veil. As much as I wish for my freedom, I now face a harsh reality: death just might be my only escape.

5

LUCA

Even after a few hours of restless sleep, my mind remains tangled with conflicting thoughts about Olivia. She caught me off guard last night, in more ways than one. More than once and more than I was comfortable with.

As the leader of Monroe Investments, I have always prided myself on staying ten steps ahead of those around me. But Olivia has managed to infiltrate my thoughts, creating a perplexing mixture of attraction and frustration within me. The mere notion of a woman having this effect on me makes her not only a liability but also a significant risk.

The innocence she had initially portrayed has been contradicted by her disobedient nature, and the temptation to rid myself of this problem is strong. Yet, I find myself hesitating, grappling with emotions that I'm unaccustomed to.

Still, I know that I can't afford to let her burrow further under my skin.

Sitting in my office at home, my contemplation continues until Jaxon knocks at my door.

"Come in," I say, pushing aside the papers I wasn't really reading.

Jaxon steps into the room, his golden eyes appraising me respectfully as he closes the door behind him. "The news is reporting on Senator McAdams."

I lean forward, my curiosity piqued. "And?"

"They're saying it's a robbery gone wrong," he explains before sitting down across from me. "The FBI is taking over the investigation, but they have no suspects."

A flicker of annoyance rises within me but doesn't last long. "If Damon did his job, then we shouldn't have anything to worry about."

Damon, one of my most trusted associates, possesses the skills to ensure that no trace of our involvement is left behind in any situation. He has always been meticulous in covering our tracks, diverting attention away from our operations.

"What are we going to do about the securities bill McAdams was pushing through?" Jaxon asks, reminding me that I have somewhere to be soon.

A hint of a smile tugs at the corners of my lips. "We'll resort to blackmail if necessary. None of those politicians are clean. We'll still get what we need."

Jaxon's expression turns serious as he raises an intriguing possibility. "What if Moretti was trying to prevent the bill from passing? He might have orchestrated the senator's death to create chaos."

I raise a brow. "Why would you say that?"

"Because these are scenarios you pay me to consider." The cocky smirk on his face is nothing I can argue with.

While I don't appreciate when Jaxon questions my motives, like with Olivia, he is the person I trust most to make me consider all aspects of a decision, even if he doesn't always do that for himself.

He gestures around the room. "You've always been more powerful than Moretti. Yes, he's been amicable with our boundaries, but that doesn't mean he hasn't been plotting. No alliance is set in stone, Luc. You know this better than anyone."

That I do. Unfortunately, my father didn't, and I've learned from his mistakes since taking over more than a decade ago.

Titan Moretti wouldn't be the first idiot to come against my family, but there's a reason that Monroe Investments is the wealthiest corporation on the West Coast—maybe even the United States.

People don't fuck with us and get away with it.

"We need to tread carefully," I say. "Let's gather more information before jumping to conclusions. Assign Markus and Damon to discreetly find intel about Moretti's involvement. I don't want to provoke conflict if there are other factors at play. But also, be ready. I'm not afraid of this escalating quickly."

When I'd arrived in the alleyway last night, McAdams was already dead, and it was less than a minute later that Olivia walked out. I'll need to put a call into Titan to see why his men were even there. Though, he'll expect an update on Olivia, and I'm not going to give him one. At least not the one he wants.

An idea hits me square in the chest. One that just may be exactly what I need to keep Moretti in check.

"Titan won't act drastically, though," I add with a smirk. "We have the woman. There's a reason he wants her dead. She's not a liability. She's a *witness*."

Jaxon lips flatten. "A witness that has seen a lot here already. Too much, in fact. But that's the least of our problems when it comes to your guest. Have you done anything about her absence from the world? Unless you already know that nobody will miss her, we should probably do something to prevent people from searching for her."

Fuck. How could I have overlooked such a crucial detail? The reminder that this woman has begun to fester within my mind irritates me to no end.

"Damon should have taken care of retrieving her belongings when he handled the scene," I reply, regaining my composure and pushing aside my continued frustration. "Tell Justine to reply to any new messages on Olivia's behalf, at least until she becomes more compliant. Justine can earn the woman's trust and get her to do what we want. Either that, or I'll make her see reason."

The image of pinning Olivia against the wall, showing her the darkness I'm capable of with just one look, is much too appealing to act on just yet. For now, Jaxon's girlfriend Justine can be of use.

He prepares to leave, rising from his seat. "Want me to have her bring food to Olivia as well?"

My fingers push together, steepling in front of me. I want to tell him no, but this could be better. My absence should help Olivia understand that she doesn't hold any power and that I'm not going to be the man who rescues her from that cell.

No, when I choose to set her free, she'll be mine to command, a mere pawn in the world I've spent my entire life constructing.

Though, even as I think the words, it's as if a knife twists in my chest. The idea of reducing this particular woman to nothing more than property causes a momentary unease within me that I'm not accustomed to.

That knowledge gives me my final answer. "Yes, but," my gaze levels on him, "make sure Justine understands that Olivia isn't to be released for any reason. Not to piss or shit or see the sun. If she disobeys—"

"Understood, Boss," Jaxon cuts in, his voice laced with the unwavering loyalty I've always known from him. "Justine's been here a few months now. She knows the rules, and she hasn't pushed a single boundary in that time."

No, she hasn't. Another thing that has surprised me as of late.

"Make sure Olivia has breakfast and dinner," I add. "No lunch. I won't be back until tonight after I've appeased the board members that the Senator's death doesn't pose a threat to Monroe Investments."

Not only do I intend to do that, but I also hope to rid my mind of the image of Olivia's creamy skin and fuckable lips.

At least until she's compliant in more ways than one. It hasn't gone unnoticed that she's just as affected by my presence, if not more, as I am to hers. Though, she might also be as stubborn, but I'm prepared for that. Whatever game we end up playing, I don't intend on losing.

This raven is mine to cage. Her fate was decided the moment she stepped into the alleyway.

Maybe even before that.

6

OLIVIA

Begrudgingly, I must admit that the mattress Luca left for me is like sleeping on a cloud. Even without the box spring and frame beneath its soft surface, I was lulled to sleep within minutes after being left alone.

As I wake, I assume it's the following morning, but given darkness still engulfs my surroundings, it's not possible to even guess at the time. The cell's concrete walls and floors still emanate a cold chill, but my current predicament outweighs any discomfort I feel.

I desperately need to pee. Like really fucking badly.

Luca mentioned there was a bucket in here, but I haven't located it yet. I don't want to. The idea of relieving myself in a tin can feels degrading on so many levels. Sure, I've peed in the woods before, but this is inhumane.

After futilely rocking back and forth on the mattress for several agonizing minutes, I mutter under my breath, "Fuck it."

Summoning my resolve, I rise to my feet and feel along the wall, using it as a guide to navigate my cell. With each step, I cautiously sweep my foot, hoping to find the elusive bucket in the darkness.

Soon enough, my boot collides with metal, eliciting a cringe from myself. "Am I really doing this?" I question, and the confirmation swiftly echoes back from my desperate bladder.

I position the bucket between my legs, using my hands to blindly feel around the top, making sure there isn't anything I have to look out for. Nobody needs something stabbing them in the ass first thing in the morning.

Satisfied that I'm in the clear, I unbutton my jeans and assume a squatting position. Before I can even confirm that the bucket is in place, my body begins relieving itself. Seems my impatient bladder couldn't wait a second more.

No longer embarrassed to be using the bucket, I finish my business and stand up. My pants are still at my ankles when I hear a key enter the lock of my cell door, causing panic to course through me.

Fuck. How did I miss the sound of Luca's heavy footsteps?

In my frantic attempt to cover myself, my lowered jeans cause me to trip, and I crash onto the unforgiving concrete, my knees taking the brunt of the impact.

On the bright side, I manage to avoid landing on the bucket filled with my urine. However, any fleeting sense of triumph quickly dissipates as the cell door swings open, exposing my bare ass to whoever is on the other side.

"Well, hello there," a woman's voice chimes in with a chuckle. "Jaxon told me you were feisty, but I didn't expect this kind of greeting."

Mother fuck fuck.

I scramble to sit upright, my face burning with embarrassment as I hastily pull up my jeans and turn to face the woman who has invaded my private humiliation.

With a mix of curiosity and amusement, she steps further into the cell, revealing herself in the dim light from the hallway. Her eyes sparkle mischievously, and a playful smile dances over her lips. I can't deny that there's an air of confidence about her, as if she's completely at ease in this unconventional situation.

"Sorry about that," I stammer, feeling my cheeks flush even hotter. "I didn't expect anyone to come in."

"You have nothing to worry about with me," she replies, her voice carrying a sincere and calming tone that begins to ease my racing heart. "I'm Justine and you're Olivia, yeah?"

I nod, my relief mingled with confusion, preventing any coherent words from escaping my lips. My eyes involuntarily fixate on the plate she holds in her hands. I let the tantalizing aroma of the sandwich, the glistening bottle of water, and the sight of freshly cut pineapple overwhelm my senses for the moment.

"Jaxon—that's my boyfriend—sent me down here to

bring you food," she says, extending the plate to me. "I know it's early, but I'm not much of a cook, and I thought you might appreciate a real sandwich instead of toast."

Her words strike a chord. She's right. The previous night, thanks to my nerves before the auction, I couldn't bring myself to eat dinner. My stomach growls, responding to the mere sight of the food. With one hand holding the plate, I use the other to reach for the sandwich, not even bothering to check its contents before devouring the sustenance.

As I take the first bite, soft, fresh bread melts in my mouth, sending waves of satisfaction through me. I can't help but moan in delight. "Good God, that's delicious."

Justine chuckles, leaning casually against the doorway. "I'm glad," she says, her amusement evident. Then, her gaze sweeps around the cell. "This is the first time I've actually looked inside one of these since moving in."

I gape at her, a mixture of astonishment and curiosity taking hold of me. "You live *here*?"

She nods with a sense of pride. "This is the kind of family that you're either all in with or not at all," she admits, her voice tinged with a touch of something I don't comprehend.

"Are you here by force?" I ask, even though she looks happy. That doesn't mean she hasn't been coerced.

Her head rears back. "God no." Then, she grins. "Well, maybe for the first ten minutes, but then I realized being with this mafia is safer than being on my own. At least, it was when I first arrived. Still, I love it here now. A little lonely at times, but I wouldn't change a thing. At least not yet."

As I chew my third bite, my mind attempts to process the information she's just shared, but the overload of emotions has me focusing on Justine's appearance instead of her words.

She's striking with dark, fiery red hair flowing past her shoulders and bright hazel eyes that distract me from my current reality. She's tall, probably several inches in height on me, and dressed casually in jeans, black, strappy sandals, and green tank top. There's an undeniable aura of self-assurance around her that both intrigues and intimidates me.

However, the diversion provided by her presence is short-lived as the weight of just one of her previously spoken words finally forces its way to the forefront of my thoughts.

Mafia.

The word echoes relentlessly in my mind. This is Portland, Oregon—a city known for its vibrant culture, diverse cuisines, and artistic expression. But a mafia? That seems inconceivable, almost comical.

Yet, the events of last night flood back into my consciousness. The sight of a lifeless body, the shots fired in my direction, and the enigmatic man in the designer suit who stole me away to this underground cell. Panic begins to claw at my throat, tightening its hold with each passing second.

Oh, God. I've been kidnapped by the mafia.

The realization hits me like a freight train, and I feel a chill run down my spine. My mind races, trying to make sense of it all, to understand how I ended up in this situation.

Justine's gaze softens as if she can read the turmoil in my eyes. She takes a step closer, her voice gentle but resolute. "I know it's overwhelming. But you're safe here. Luca may be the boss and scary as fuck at times, but he won't harm you. Well, not unless you pose a threat to his family or the business."

Swallowing my next bite becomes a meticulous process, each chew feeling like a desperate attempt to grind away the lump lodged in my throat. With trepidation, I summon the courage to utter my next words. "He said I was a liability. Put me in this cell. I'm pretty sure he already thinks of me as a threat."

Justine's laughter fills the air once more, carefree and mirthful, and a pang of jealousy stabs at me. "Oh, honey. If that were true, you wouldn't still be breathing. You'd be in a dumpster downtown somewhere or at the bottom of the Columbia."

Fucking hell. Her words do nothing to ease the knot of anxiety tightening within me.

She continues, "But don't repeat that I told you that. I shouldn't have even mentioned the mafia, but that's something you could have put together on your own after what you saw. Regardless, even though I love Jaxon and would never turn on him, they forced you here, and you should at least know what you're dealing with. Plus, I can trust you, right?"

There's a bit of a darkness that passes over her face at that last question, and something tells me Justine isn't always as bubbly as she's portrayed so far. Still, I nod as I consider everything she's shared, even though she knows she shouldn't.

The hunger that once consumed me dissipates as I do, replaced by a heavy weight that settles in my chest. Setting the half-eaten plate on the mattress, I realize I no longer have an appetite. "You're seriously happy here?" I ask, my voice laced with bewilderment.

Justine's expression grows pensive, her gaze locking with mine in a moment of shared empathy and understanding. "I won't deny there are risks, and the word 'mafia' carries a certain...distaste, but it's not like they're prowling the streets every night, searching for people to murder. They're businessmen, to some extent. They avoid violence when they can and possess an unwavering loyalty. Knowing what Jaxon has done for me and what he would do in the future to ensure my safety... I choose to find solace in that knowledge, not fear."

I'm left speechless. There's no understanding the world she's describing, or perhaps I simply refuse to. I don't want to be the kind of woman who seeks comfort in the act of taking another person's life.

"I'm glad you're happy here," I manage to say, struggling to maintain a respectful tone. "But I didn't end up in this situation by choice. My life is...complicated right now. I need to find a way out of here before I lose everything."

My words carry not only the weight of my own life hanging by a thread but also the burden of my mother's house. The sole reason I found myself in that damn hotel last night was to earn the money that would secure her home. If I were to lose it all despite my efforts... I can't even fathom the thought.

"Oh, speaking of," she says, then reaches into her back pocket and wiggles my phone between her fingers. "I need your passcode so we can make sure nobody calls the police to report you missing."

I raise both of my brows in surprise. Not only because my phone is supposed to be missing, but because I don't understand why in hell they would think I'd comply with that request?

Not only would I prefer someone to report me missing, but the phone holds important details of my life that someone like Luca Monroe doesn't need to be privy to.

Justine exhales wearily, her arm dropping to her side in defeat. "Listen, Olivia. I know we're strangers, but try to think of me as your friend. I'm here to make things easier for you, to help you escape this cage. But in order for me to do that, you need to trust me."

That's the second time she's mentioned the word "trust," and while she seems almost too easy to talk to, I don't know that I can right now. The concept feels foreign in this dim, desolate space. I cast a skeptical glance around, my gaze taking in the walls that hold me captive. Believing in any of these people? It's a notion seemingly as fictional as the situation I find myself in should be.

Justine's voice cuts through my doubts, her tone earnest and pleading. "If you refuse, if you yell or threaten, you'll only prolong your stay here, possibly for weeks or months. I won't be able to help you. But if you comply, if you show them that you're not a threat, regardless of what you've witnessed, then I can get you out of here."

Her words hang in the air, accompanied by a sense of desperation and grief that clouds my judgment. Perhaps it's the turmoil I've been hurled into, distorting my perceptions and warping my capacity for reason. How else could I find even a flicker of attraction toward the monster who threw me into this abyss?

I take a moment to contemplate her proposition. Her sincerity resonates within me, and despite the whirlwind of emotions and the fog of uncertainty, a glimmer of hope begins to emerge. Maybe, just maybe, I can find a way to navigate this treacherous terrain.

"Fine," I concede, extending my hand toward her. "Give me my phone, and I'll show you my email and texts."

The grimace that appears on her face tells me everything I don't want to know.

"I know I just said I'm your friend, but there are certain things I can't do until I'm told otherwise," she explains, tone full of sympathy. "You can't have your phone, but I promise, if you give me the passcode, I'll be respectful of your privacy and I'll relay anything you need to know. I can even read your messages aloud for you, if you want. But without the code, they'll remain locked."

Damn it. I hope this isn't a mistake I'll come to regret.

With a sigh that carries the weight of defeat, I reluctantly reveal, "It's six-three-eight-seven."

Her returning smile isn't one of triumph, but rather full of understanding and shared sorrow, offering me a modicum of solace against the aching void within my chest.

"Oh, God," she gasps only a second after unlocking my phone. Her hand covers her mouth as tears shimmer in her eyes. "There's a message here... Your mom..."

"I already know," I reply, my voice heavy with resignation. "She passed away last week."

A strangled curse escapes her lips, laden with a mix of anger and grief. "Fuck. And now you're... I'm so sorry, Olivia."

I shrug, a gesture born out of helplessness. What else is there to do? I attempted to fight back in my own way, and it only led me to an underground cell.

She returns the phone to her pocket, stepping closer until our hands meet, her grip enveloping mine with warmth and determination. "We're going to get you out of here. Together. I promise. Please trust me to help you."

As I peer into her hazel eyes, that previous flicker of hope I had grows a little bigger. Against all odds, I find myself nodding. I can find a way to place my faith in this stranger. Her compassion can be the lifeline I need to survive this nightmare.

Somehow, I will claw my way out of this wretched place. The despair that threatened to consume me before won't win.

Most importantly, Luca Monroe won't break me.

7

LUCA

Being in this meeting is fucking hell. The board members—men and women that know nothing of my underground business or how I always get what I want—are up my ass about the Senator's death. They know we have—or had—a close connection, but not because of anything more than the Senator looking for a generous donation to his next campaign that will now never happen.

I pinch the bridge of my nose and hold in my snarl. "I told you, I will handle this."

"But how?" Steven demands. "Without that securities bill, the investments we've made for our clients are at risk. Millions of dollars could be lost, Luca. Do you not understand how important it is to make sure that doesn't happen?"

My palm comes down harder on the table than I intend it to. "Considering I built this company and hand-chose every single one of you, I'm rather certain I *understand* perfectly fine, Steven." We lock stares and, as I expect, he looks down first. "As I said a dozen times already, I will fix this. The rest of you need to only concern yourselves with the acquisitions you pushed on the company that are currently failing."

Monroe Investments not only does financial investing, but we also buy other companies silently, build them back, and profit on our success. Yet, when a few of the board members pushed for us to get involved with a shipping company, I didn't realize how idiotic they truly were.

The whole thing has been a loss, thanks to the mule of an owner. And now, he's one month away from losing everything, per the contract he signed when Monroe Investments handed him several million dollars to buy new trucks and boats with.

But it's not all bad. At least if I have hands fully on the company, I can use it however I see fit, which may help other dealings the board members don't need to know about.

Nobody else says anything and I take another glance at my phone, knowing I need to get the hell out of here before I actually stab someone.

I push away from the table and stand from my chair. "One last time for those not listening before." I level my hardened gaze on each of the eight members. "The securities bill will pass. Just because I'm not here as much as you assume I should be doesn't mean I'm not always working on other solutions to keep my company running as I know it's capable of doing."

I walk out of the room before anyone else can piss me off and head straight downstairs where Damon is waiting for me in the SUV.

He doesn't ask how my day was or if I'm okay. He merely drives back to Monroe, and for that I'm thankful.

My phone vibrates with a new text.

Titan: You still haven't sent proof of dealing with the problem.

Me: And I'm not going to until I know she's no longer of use to me.

He should be wondering why she might be useful and if he's smart, he'll know that I'm not against using this woman against him. By his lack of response, I assume he's figured that out on his own.

Within twenty minutes, we're back at Roe compound, and Damon opens my door for me as I finish checking emails from the Vice President of Accounts over at Monroe. It's another negative update on Sutton Transport. I'm not the least bit surprised.

As I get out of the vehicle, phone still in hand, I consider checking on Olivia from the video feed I have access to on my phone, but I decide better of it. She might be a temptation that I'm drawn to, but I still have control, and just maybe she's also figured that out in the time I've been gone.

I don't want to keep her in a cage, but I will if she insists on being insolent. Not only to assert my dominance but also to demonstrate to those who work here where my priorities lay. I trust them to remain loyal, but any inkling of doubt regarding my focus and determination could be detrimental.

Damon stays at the car and reopens the driver's door. "I have somewhere to be unless you need me for anything."

I glance over at him and can't read a single emotion on his face. "No. Enjoy your night."

He isn't one of my men that I keep tabs on. I haven't had a need to. One phone call and that man is always there, without question, doing as I ask. He can have his secrets as long as he keeps mine in return.

I head toward the elevator. Once I step inside, my finger hesitates for the briefest of seconds before pressing the button for level one.

Olivia won't be the first person I go to once I get home.

No, I think I'll head to the kitchen, grab dinner, and take a scalding shower to wash the day off me before checking in.

However, as I step out of the elevator and see Jaxon waiting for me, I know that's not all going to be possible.

"What's wrong now?" I ask, annoyance simmering within me at the prospect of returning home to more complications after the chaos at the office.

"Have you been to see Olivia yet?" he asks, hands casually tucked into his pockets.

"No." I brush past him, expecting if he has more to say, then he'll follow.

I remove my suitcoat and toss it over a chair before turning toward the refrigerator. Seeing Jaxon in my peripherals has my fingers tightening around the cool handles.

"Is there something I need to know?" I ask, voice tinged with skepticism.

"Her mother died," he starts, and a hollow emptiness seeps into my chest.

Have I inadvertently been keeping that woman from her family when they need her?

"Apparently, Olivia was only at that auction to earn some money to pay the bills left behind after the death," Jaxon continues, alleviating some of the guilt that she missed an opportunity to say goodbye to her mother.

Though, other ideas fill my mind due to this new information, but I don't voice them.

"And this matters to me why?" I ask, relinquishing my grip on the refrigerator and turning back toward him. As far as Jaxon should be concerned—after our earlier conversation—Olivia is nothing more than a chess piece to me. I'm keeping her alive as leverage against Titan. A witness to keep him in check.

"Just thought you may want to know before speaking with her again," Jaxon replies, his shoulders taking on a rigidity. "It may be factoring into how she's responding to all of this."

"What else did Justine learn?" I ask, because Jaxon has a point. I need to know Olivia better before I see her again if I have any hope of her complying in the ways I need.

"Her only family was her mother," he says. "She has one friend she talks to most named Tori and co-worker

Sandi, who has reached out but doesn't seem overly concerned. Tori, though, has called over a dozen times and texted twice as many since we took the woman. Justine said with Olivia's help that she handled the messages, but either one of them could pose a problem later. Olivia has a job as an accountant for some warehouse, which she isn't too fond of. No allergies and really fucking hates you."

A smirk creeps across my face at that last statement. One I'm certain he's delivered more as my friend than as one of my employees.

"Good," I reply, satisfaction dripping from my voice. "She should hate me, but that doesn't mean she can't see reason. I have a plan, and it's going to work. Olivia isn't going to be a problem. In fact, I predict she's going to prevent several unfortunate circumstances."

I go back to gathering my previously prepared dinner and hear Jaxon's retreating footsteps. I know he doesn't agree with my decisions, but I don't give a fuck. He's not the one that turned Monroe Investments into a multi-billion-dollar company instead of a façade of a business used to front the family's dirty money, and I did that while also making every fool lurking in the shadows think twice before coming after us.

Well, all except for possibly Titan Moretti, and if he thinks he can take what's mine from me, I'll be the first to remind him of who the fuck I am. Keeping Olivia alive is just one step in doing so.

———

I finish my dinner, savoring every bite before I relax under the scalding hot shower that washes away the remnants of the day. I change into fresh clothes, a tailored suit that exudes power and authority, something I believe Olivia will need constant reminders of.

As I stride toward her cell, a familiar air of control settles around me for the first time since entering that alleyway. This woman is nothing more than a means to an end, a pawn in this dangerous game, and now that I have a clear understanding of that end—using her to keep Titan from starting a war he can't win—my priorities feel more secure.

I stop at the metal door holding Olivia hostage, the faint sound of my footsteps echoing in the enclosed space. With a steadying breath, I unlock the door and shove it open with force.

My eyes search the darkness, and it takes a moment to find her in the furthest corner, huddled on the mattress.

Her legs uncurl, and she pushes herself into a standing position, but it's not a defiant move. No, this almost seems respectful.

Maybe Justine has been more helpful than I could have predicted.

Olivia's guarded gaze remains fixed on me as I lean against the doorframe, observing her every move. I wait, allowing the silence to stretch between us, curious to see if she'll break first.

After a moment of contemplation, she lets out a

heavy sigh, as if burdened by my mere presence. She gives me her back and takes a step toward the mattress.

Not wanting to lose her attention, I forfeit the silence first before she can sit back down. "Allowing Justine to use your phone was a welcome display of cooperation. I didn't expect that from you, but I appreciate it nonetheless."

She pauses, her back still turned to me, and seems to contemplate her response. "I didn't really think I had a choice," she finally admits, her voice tinged with resignation.

"You always have a choice, Little Raven." My words are meant to be sincere, but they seem to echo louder within the confines of the cell than intended.

There's a hitch in her shoulders, and her head drops ever so slightly. "Cooperate or die. That's a hell of a choice."

Her tone holds no malice, unlike our previous conversations. She seems dejected, which is... disappointing.

I maintain my firm tone, refusing to let her doubts undermine my authority. "Regardless, you made the right one. You have a purpose here, and until it's been served, cooperating with me will remain the best option."

Her head half turns back toward me, her expression the epitome of disbelief. "The best option for who? I highly doubt any of this will benefit me, in any way, in the end."

With a calculated move, I step into the shadows of the wretched room, closing the distance between us. The proximity electrifies the air, creating an undeniable tension between us.

My body hovers mere inches from hers, and I lower my head, whispering into her ear. "For both of us. Do you grasp the gravity of what you witnessed in that alley? Those men intended to end your life, and just because they failed once doesn't mean they won't try again. You can despise me and resent the situation I've forced upon you, but make no mistake, I'm saving your life while securing what I want."

A shudder runs through her body, betraying a mix of fear and uncertainty. Her voice trembles as she asks, "And what is it that you want?"

"That's not for you to know," I assert, pausing to ensure she's listening intently. "As I mentioned earlier, your cooperation is appreciated, and you have earned yourself another luxury. However, it will need to be revealed tomorrow."

Now that I'm confident she has grasped her situation, it's not my intention to leave her a prisoner. For her, it may seem like a lose-lose situation, but given time, she will come to realize that I'm not the worst monster she could have been entangled with.

She lifts her head higher, our bodies still in close proximity, and her eyes flicker with renewed determination. "Who were those men in the alley?"

Her question catches me off guard, not expecting her to steer the conversation in that direction. It takes a moment for me to respond, her breath gently caressing my face as her eyes search mine, yearning for answers I'm certain she won't find.

"They were men you've never heard of before," I finally reply, staring down at her with unwavering intensity. "But rest assured, they now possess all the information they need to know about you, Olivia Danes. Just as I do. However, unlike them, I won't use that information to end you."

A hint of uncertainty creeps into her voice as she presses further. "How am I supposed to know that? How can I trust that if I keep cooperating that you won't kill me anyway or hurt those that I care about?"

My gaze hardens, and I inch my face closer to hers, our breaths mingling in the tense atmosphere. "You won't know, and you shouldn't trust anyone other than yourself," I declare, my voice laced with harsh reality.

She may not have wanted to hear that, but it's the truth and I don't often make a liar out of myself. Just because I'm keeping her alive doesn't mean I won't hurt her, and I won't promise otherwise.

She finally takes a step back. "Understood."

As she retreats, I know I've overstayed. Not because the raven before me no longer wishes for me to be in her presence, but because the walls and reasons I'd intentionally focused on today during my time away are beginning to falter.

I cannot care for this woman. She is a means to an end. Nothing more and plenty less. Protecting all I've built is the only thing I need to focus on.

Not the fact that even though she could have

attempted to guilt me into a million things, given her circumstances and the passing of her mother, she hasn't.

She's been defiant, but she hasn't truly fought me. I need to keep that fact far from my thoughts, because understanding why just might be the thing that gets her killed.

8

OLIVIA

Admitting defeat keeps me from sleeping well the night before, but when Justine returns the following morning with breakfast, I'm determined to remain strong. I won't let Luca Monroe break me. I'll play his game, and I'll find a way to win. I have to.

"Good morning, sunshine," Justine says cheerily as she enters my cell. I immediately notice a cart behind her, holding more than just eggs and bacon that the house cook apparently prepared this time. The aroma of freshly brewed coffee wafts in the air, mingling with the scent of warm pastries. "I brought a few things to make your... space more friendly." She throws a roll of toilet paper and some hand sanitizer at me. "Figured these would make you the happiest."

Oh, how right she is. I clutch the precious items to my chest. "You're an angel."

She grimaces, and lines form around her downturned

mouth. "That's not true. If I were, then you wouldn't still be in here. I'd have helped you escape already."

I tilt my head to the side, studying her. "But I thought you said this place wasn't as bad as I was making it out to be."

Had I misunderstood her before and my compliance with Luca is misplaced?

"It's not a bad place for *me*," she says, her voice tinged with a hint of mischief. "But I realize that you're not me, and nobody should have to stay where they don't want to be. The only reason I'm not risking Luca's wrath for you is because Jaxon told me what would happen if you left too soon."

Luca previously mentioned that men would gladly kill me because of what I saw, but he refused to say anything further. Maybe Justine will be willing to elaborate for me. The more I know, the more I can take back control of my life.

"Yeah, the men from the alleyway... Wouldn't want them to kill me," I say without confidence, already failing at my subterfuge. And here I keep telling myself that I can win against Luca. *Right.*

Justine pulls out a battery-operated lamp and clicks it on, casting a warm glow in the previously dimly lit cell. Her hazel eyes stand out brighter than I've yet to see, and her dark red hair holds a stunning sheen as it falls in waves around her shoulders. "I should have brought this yesterday, but hopefully it will help now."

"Luca mentioned last night that I've earned another

freedom thanks to my cooperation with my phone," I say. "Is all this part of that?"

She frowns, her eyes narrowing with displeasure. "No. I didn't hear anything of the sort, and what a dick for making you *earn* what was stolen from you. I know I said you should cooperate to make things easier, but...I swear some days I don't know whether I want to stab that man or praise him."

A frown forms between my eyes as confusion clouds my thoughts. "Praise him? What could Luca Monroe possibly deserve *praise* for?"

Justine offers me a saucy wink, her glossy lips curving upward. "That, my dear, you're going to have to learn on your own. Just trust me when I say you're safest here, and your continued cooperation will get you out of here. One way or another, even if I have to make sure of it myself."

My new friend pulls a pillow from the cart next, followed by a toothbrush and paste, a comb with a hair tie wrapped around the handle, and more water bottles than I'll probably drink since I'm not a fan of peeing in that godforsaken bucket.

"Can you think of anything else you might need to make this more...tolerable?" she asks, sincerity lacing her words. "I was specifically instructed not to let you leave and to get you to cooperate, but they never said I couldn't bring presents."

I'm liking Justine more and more as I get to know her. She's wild—the complete opposite of my best friend Tori —but she has the confidence of my co-worker Sandi, which brings me comfort in a small way.

"If it's not too much," I hesitate, feeling a twinge of vulnerability. The odds of finding art supplies in this place are slim to none. "Never mind. No, this is all really great. Thank you so much."

She crosses her arms and narrows her eyes on me, her gaze penetrating. "What do you want, Olivia? I'm not afraid to tell you no if it's not possible. But more importantly, you shouldn't be afraid to ask for what you want. The worst that can happen is you don't get it, and nothing has changed, but what if, and this applies to all things in life, you do get what you want and everything changes?"

Given her snarky attitude, I didn't expect something profound to leave her lips, but damn, her words hit me like a punch to the gut.

Justine moves closer and places her hand on my shoulder, her touch both comforting and empowering. "Hope can always be found in the darkness. No matter how shitty things might be right now with losing your mom and ending up here, never give up. There is always something to focus on that can give you the strength to survive, and I'm going to expect nothing less than your best, Olivia Danes. You fight that fucker with all you have."

Hope in the darkness... Considering I've been living in literal darkness for what feels like days, instead of the hours I'm sure it's been, those words are exactly what I need to hear.

"You want me to fight back against Luca now?" I ask,

because that goes against what she's already told me to do to survive here.

She shakes her head and smirks, hazel eyes glinting with pride. "Not in the way you're thinking. You need to fight in a way that only a woman knows how."

A lump forms in my throat as I grasp her meaning. "I'm not sleeping with him."

"And you don't have to, but that doesn't mean you can't make him want you." She waves a hand over my disheveled appearance. "Smeared makeup, tangled hair, dirtied sweatshirt, and jeans be damned, you're stunning. Even better, you already have Luca wrapped around your finger. You just need to learn how to make him sing. Now, tell me what else you want that can bring a little sunshine to this pit of despair."

I blink several times, struggling to comprehend what she's said. *I* have Luca wrapped around *my* finger? I want to laugh, but the reality of my captivity weighs heavily on me. I'm locked down here, and he's had his hands around my throat more than once, threatening my life. However, I don't remind her of any of that.

"Painting is what I do when I'm overly stressed," I confess, my voice filled with longing. "Even if it's just a pencil and paper to sketch on, that would mean a lot to me."

An art set was the last present my father gave me before he disappeared. I thought it was ridiculous at the time, but after he was gone...I found solace in the brush strokes and kept learning how to be better. Looking back on it now, I'm pretty sure my child-self was merely trying to be good enough for him to come back home. While I find that asinine now, I'm still grateful for the outlet and have no desire to give it up even though my father gave up on me.

"Oh, girl." Justine embraces me tightly, her warmth and genuine care enveloping me. "You are too precious for this world. I'll be back down with some more things soon."

I hug her back, and I instinctively know that this dynamic woman is going to be my hope in this darkness. It doesn't matter what Luca says or does. Even after only three interactions with her, I feel confident Justine is going to be someone I can trust, which gives me a confidence that just maybe I'll survive this hellhole.

———

Hours have passed, and I find myself in a surprisingly content state. Seated on the mattress, I rest against the new pillow, my legs snugly wrapped in the blanket. The battery-operated lamp is on the cool floor beside me, casting a soft glow on the surroundings. With a pencil grasped between my fingers, I've immersed myself in the world of art, thanks to the items Justine returned with.

She didn't have paint but promised to get some ordered. Secretly, I hope I'm not here long enough to receive anything that needs to be ordered. Though, that's likely nothing more than wishful thinking.

I press the charcoal tip firmly against the paper, creating bold lines that I then smudge with the side of my thumb, blending them to my satisfaction. Gradually, I transition to lighter strokes, adjusting the angle of my wrist with each movement, until the image on the page starts to come alive.

I remember hearing that visualization can be a powerful tool for manifesting desires in life. Inspired by Justine's empowering words, I decide to draw what I long for, allowing time to slip away as I pour my heart into the sketch. As I gaze at the final result, I can't deny that it's far from perfect, but it carries the essence of what I need.

The scene depicts me kneeling in my mother's once-vibrant garden, now lost to neglect. Yet, in my drawing, I visualize its revival, a tribute to my mother's memory. Above me, the radiant sun beams down, and I can almost feel its warmth, as though my mother's love is embracing me from above.

Emotions surge within me, a mixture of longing and sorrow that threaten to overwhelm. I close my eyes, clenching my fists, fighting back the tears that beg to cascade down my cheeks. "I miss you so fucking much, Mom," I whisper, the words heavy with pain.

I lean my head back against the pillow, holding the drawing to my chest, desperately clinging to the hope that I will escape this wretched place. This can't be the end for me—I refuse to believe it.

A renewed determination surges through me, fueled by Justine's unwavering support. Yet, even in my newfound resolve, the ache and fear remain.

While Luca previously mentioned that I've earned another freedom, he's yet to return to my cell, and that hasn't gone unnoticed. I try to convince myself that his absence is a positive sign, but with each passing moment, doubt gnaws at the edges of my hope. However, I won't let it consume me. Justine's advice echoes in my mind, a reminder that I must play the game, and not merely as a participant, but as a victor.

After a few more moments of solace with my first drawing, I flip the page and start anew. This time focusing on the flowers I intend to replant. Though, that only desperately makes me miss my paints.

The vibrancy and life that my acrylics bring to the canvas are the reason I can get so lost in the art when my heart is hurting. Yet today it's the dark strokes of the pencil that I must focus on.

Once I'm done, I appraise the soft round petals and picture the deep pink they should be, inhaling deeply, imagining the sweet scent they'll provide in my yard one day.

A true smile graces my lips for the first since before the auction and my heart feels lighter. Yes, this is what I needed.

I'm halfway into turning the page to start on another image when the echo of footfalls sounds in the hallway, heavier than Justine's. The sound has my heart rate rising and I tuck the drawing behind me, not wanting Luca to take something so precious from me.

The lock disengages, but I stay on the bed, refusing to

show him more respect than he deserves. At least until Justine's advice whispers through my mind, reminding me that I have a game to play here. No, not just play. One I need to win.

Making sure the pad of paper is still hidden, I stand next to the mattress just as the steel door swings open.

Luca's dark eyes sweep across my cell, his expression devoid of any trace of approval. "Where did all of this come from?" he demands, his tone laced with irritation.

Great. He's going to be furious with Justine and she won't be able to see me anymore. I want to lie and cover for her, but I don't know who else I could blame.

"Never mind." He reaches for my wrist. "Come with me."

I attempt to keep my feet rooted to the ground, to deny him the obedience he demands. But my body betrays me, and I stumble forward, colliding with Luca's side. His grip tightens around my wrist, causing my arm to twist awkwardly, sending a sharp pang through my shoulder as I fall.

"Fuck," I hiss, wincing at the sudden jolt.

With quick reflexes, Luca wraps his other arm around my waist, hauling my clumsy ass back up. Once I'm standing on my own again, his finger lifts my chin and for a brief moment, I think he's going to ask if I'm hurt.

"Be fucking careful," he admonishes, his sneer erasing any remnants of the unexpected attraction his touch momentarily sparked.

"Then, don't manhandle me," I snap back without meaning to.

"Maybe it's not time for you to leave yet," he muses, and I mentally smack myself.

Play the fucking game, Danes.

I brush a hand pointlessly over my filthy clothes. "I'm sorry. That hurt, and I have a headache, and..."

His hard stare tells me he doesn't give a single fuck about my reasons, so I let the sentence trail off.

He releases me and points toward the door. "Out."

I nod, playing the obedient woman he seems to need me to be. I stand in the hallway, waiting for him to lead the rest of the way.

As he walks in front of me toward the elevator doors we previously came through, I wonder where we're going, but I keep my mouth shut. Instead, my gaze involuntarily drifts to his back, observing the way his charcoal suit molds perfectly to his form, accentuating his broad shoulders. The hem of his pants hovers just above his impeccably polished dress shoes.

Inadvertently, as he presses the button to call the elevator, raising his suitcoat with the action, I catch sight of his firm ass. It's round, but not bubbly, and the thin fabric of his pants leaves little to the imagination. Especially when he shoves his hands into his pockets, still keeping his back to me.

I lick my lips, then snarl at myself. I need to keep my shit together. This man is my captor. He is not to be ogled or touched or anything of the sort.

In a feeble attempt to justify my actions, I recall

Justine's advice to essentially seduce the devil standing before me. But no. I refuse to succumb to temptation that shouldn't even exist considering how I've been treated.

Being obedient will have to be enough. Anything else is asking for more trouble than I need. I'm sure of it.

9

LUCA

Against the advice of Jaxon and Damon, I make the necessary arrangements to relocate Olivia into my private room. I don't think too hard on the reasons I shouldn't do this, but rather focus on the potential benefits this decision holds.

It's crucial for Olivia to remain within Roe compound while minimizing further disruption in my life. It's been made clear that there are people in her life who aren't willing to let her disappear, and Justine's texts —acting on behalf of Olivia—aren't seeming to pacify whoever these other women are to the witness.

To give her a modicum of freedom, I constructed the plan of having her reside in my own room. The apartment occupies the entirety of the fourth floor, excluding the compact landing outside the space, which is where we arrive once we exit the elevator.

A sleek, steel door—much like the one back at Olivia's cell, minus the rust—has replaced my previous one, making escape for my guest futile. Using the code on the lock, I let us into the room and step aside for Olivia to enter first.

"You're giving me a room?" she asks with disbelief and trepidation.

"No, I'm sharing my apartment with you," I reply, keeping my voice uninterested in the matter.

Her head snaps toward me, her reaction swift and forceful. "Excuse me?"

"You will stay here until further notice," I clarify, my words firm. "Unless, of course, you'd rather return to the cell."

Her eyes squeeze shut for a moment, her chest heaving with an exaggerated breath. "I'd rather not go back there."

Smirking with self-satisfaction, I reply, "I didn't think so."

Shrugging off my suitcoat, I drape it over the chair adjacent to my desk on the right before addressing the rest of the room. I gesture toward the obvious, like the living room right in front of us as well as the dining area where a small four-person oak table sits and my finger points at. "That is the only place you may eat. If I find crumbs in my bedroom or on the sofa, you'll be right back in the cell."

Her gaze scans around once again. "But no proper kitchen to make the food I'm only allowed at the table?"

"No. All meals come from downstairs," I state matter-of-factly. "Breakfast, lunch, and dinner is prepared daily by our house cook, but they only make what is necessary.

We're not wasteful, and I expect you to be considerate of that."

"You don't like wasting food, but you have no qualms about killing people. Got it." Her tone is flat, and the desire to bend her over my knee is strong, but I ignore the snide comment and move on.

"My desk back there is off limits, as is my closet," I say with authority. "You'll have access to a dresser in the bedroom."

She pauses in the doorway of my room, not seeming to understand the situation yet. "This doesn't look like a guest room."

"Because it's not," I say. "You will share my room with me. It's the only way I can keep a close eye on you without remanding you in the cell. If you don't like the thought of sleeping in the bed, feel free to pick a spot on the floor. Just know the bedding stays on the *bed*."

"And what if I try to escape while you're sleeping?" she asks with a raised brow.

"I hope you try just so you can find out the consequences of that choice," I answer, relishing in the prospect of the punishment I would undoubtedly give her. "The only bathroom is over there." I point to the furthest door on the left. "Anything you need should be available in the right set of drawers. Dirty towels get sent through the laundry chute."

She glances down at her sullied clothes, plucking at her sweatshirt. "And am I supposed to stay wrapped in a towel while I wait for these to get washed?"

The thought is appealing, but I don't intend to

torture myself *that* much. "Clothes have been brought here from your house, and you'll find enough of them in that dresser there." I nod toward the new three-drawer chest.

Her voice lowers and eyes become slits. "You went into my house?"

I face her head on, countering her challenging tone. "Is that a problem?"

There seems to be an internal fight going on within her. She wants to be furious still, but something is holding her back.

She takes a calming breath. "I guess not. Thank you."

"Don't thank me," I say. "I sent Damon. Your purse is also in the dresser. The only thing you can't have back is your phone."

Her eyes close briefly, and when she levels them on me again, she seems to force a smile onto her face. "Great."

I'm under no illusions that she considers any of this "great," but I have things to do, so I don't press for how she's truly feeling. I also can't care about that.

She ventures toward the dresser, presumably to get clothes so she can shower, and I'm ready to leave her alone, letting her figure out the rest of the boundaries I've put into place the hard way. When I step into the doorway of the bedroom, she calls out, giving me pause.

"What happens next?" she asks.

I turn slowly, bracing my hands against the doorframe. "What do you mean?"

She gestures around the spacious room. "I have a new

cell. Am I safe to assume that I'm still a prisoner, or can I earn more freedoms?"

If she wants to "earn" anything, I have no objections in letting her do so. However, her perception of the situation needs correcting.

"First, you're not a prisoner," I state firmly. "You're here for your own protection. I thought I made that clear already."

"Not a prisoner, huh?" Her brows raise high on her forehead. "You've kept me in an actual cell, then brought me here. Just because the drapes are nicer doesn't change what this is, Luca. Not to say I'm not glad to be out of the freezing cell, but I'm very much still a prisoner, regardless of the reasons you want to tell yourself that I'm here."

She's not wrong, but I'm not in the mood to have this conversation. Bringing her here already feels like a mistake and I don't make those often. Instead, I choose to remind her of what's most important at the present time.

"You'll remain here until I've leveraged your presence against Titan," I say sternly. "You're a witness to something that leaves his hands stained with blood. I intend to demonstrate for him what happens to those who attempt to sabotage my business dealings. All the while, your safety will be ensured within these walls."

"By using me?" she asks, displaying less fear than I anticipate.

"However I see fit, yes," I reply without hesitation. "I saved your life. Now you owe me."

She scoffs, but then covers the noise with a feigned

cough. "Right. And once I've repaid this...debt, what then?"

Leaving the doorway, I stalk toward her, enjoying how she backs herself against the dresser, her hands bracing themselves on the surface behind her.

My eyes roam over every inch of her form as if I already own her. She's a mess, but underneath the soiled clothes and two-day-old makeup, I can still discern her beauty. The fire in her eyes remains, despite her attempts at coyness. Her onyx-colored tresses cascade down her back, albeit tangled due to lack of care.

The temptation to touch her again, to feel the heat of her skin beneath mine, courses through me, but I restrain myself. "You want to know what happens once you've repaid your debt?" I appraise her once more, drawing out the answer while she nods and swallows hard. "You'll simply have to wait and see, Little Raven."

There's a hitch in her shoulders as her chest expands. My words render her silent, and I turn to leave the room, this time not stopping until the bedroom door is closed behind me. I linger for a moment, listening intently until I hear the open and close of the drawers, followed by the echo of her footsteps heading further from the door, presumably toward the bathroom.

The amount of satisfaction that blooms within me at knowing this woman will be sleeping in my bed tonight isn't good, but the more I'm around her, the more I seem to enjoy the torture she brings me by knowing I shouldn't touch her.

She's just as affected by me, and not just because I

frighten her. I see it in her eyes and with every breath she takes when I go near her. Fucking her would be another unexpected event that I shouldn't enjoy.

But that's not going to happen. Control isn't something I'll let myself lose with this woman. Not when I'm so intrigued by her. I'll keep her just close enough to use and protect, and when I'm done with her, she'll sign the world's most ironclad non-disclosure agreement before being shoved out the door.

That's the only solution that keeps everything moving the way it should. Olivia Danes doesn't belong in my world, and I won't give up everything I've worked toward for anyone.

Though, none of that means I can't enjoy pushing her beyond her comforts over and over again, just to see what it takes to break this woman.

10

OLIVIA

The scalding water cascades over my exhausted body, providing a soothing respite, while allowing me to relish in the sensation of warmth and cleanliness, something I vow to never take for granted again.

After I've turned off the water and wrapped a fluffy cotton towel around my body, steam fills the bathroom, continuing to warm me to my core. As I stand in front of the double-sink vanity, I reach for a smaller hand towel and use that to wipe the mirror. Once my reflection appears, I grab one of the provided makeup wipes and remove what I couldn't get in the shower.

Next, I put very minty toothpaste onto a fancy electric toothbrush. The act of brushing my teeth in front of a sink, rather than over the wretched bucket in the cell, feels remarkably refreshing.

After that and putting lotion on my face, I wring the excess water from my long locks again, then head back toward the bedroom. I crack the door open slowly in case Luca has returned from wherever he disappeared to.

Seeing him while I'm mostly naked doesn't seem like the brightest of ideas. My traitorous body reacts a little too much to my captor, and after our little chat earlier, I don't believe Luca missed that reaction.

The way he'd drug his gaze over my body as I pressed myself against the dresser... It was both infuriating and tantalizing. That makes me believe something is seriously broken in my head from the trauma of this whole situation.

Seeing a dead body, being shot at, and then kidnapped. It has all put my mind into shock, short-circuiting my thoughts and emotions. That is the only explanation for why I could be remotely attracted to that devil of a man.

He is everything that is wrong with this world. I'm sure of it.

Except...I can't help but remember the way he picked me up from the ground in that alleyway. Yes, I'm a witness he can use against someone else, but I can also be used against Luca. He should have let me die there, and he didn't.

As I walk through the room, I smack my palm against the side of my head in frustration. "Don't be a fucking idiot. The odds of me getting out of this place alive aren't high."

Unless Justine sneaks me out, but by the time it's safe for me to be out in the real world, she might not have time to get me out. It's crossed my mind more than once that when I'm no longer needed as his witness, there's nothing to stop Luca from killing me.

Though, that doesn't mean I'm not going to prepare for being able to go home. My long shower allowed me to think of the things I can't do anything about but need to find a way to act on, even while I'm locked up.

I need to ask Justine if she can deliver my wallet to Tori. The bills for my mother's house need to be paid. After everything, losing the house is a fate I refuse to accept. Tori can help make sure that doesn't happen. Though, there is a risk that my friend will ask too many questions about why I need her to do this.

I could always tell her I'm having a mental breakdown and I've escaped to the woods, but that I'll be back as soon as I'm ready to deal with life. She might buy that. Hopefully.

The other option is asking Justine to assist with more than reaching out to Tori. Though, that's asking too much of a new friend and someone who, at the end of the day, is likely to do what's best for my captor rather than me. I know she means well, but I don't expect her to put her life in jeopardy for me.

"Fuck," I mutter into the empty room as I open the first dresser drawer.

Acknowledging that having access to the amenities is preferable to solitude, I resign myself to getting dressed and finding some semblance of comfort in my new prison.

Everything else will sort itself out later. I'll keep

telling myself that until it comes true or I'm no longer able to.

———

"Olivia? Dear God, don't tell me you escaped." Justine's panicked voice jolts me awake from the comfort of Luca's bed.

My palms rub over my eyes as I call out to her. "Back here." I fell asleep after using all the luxuries provided in the bathroom. It had been three in the afternoon when I last glanced at the clock, and now it's dark out the window. Given it's summertime, it's likely well after nine in the evening.

"Shit," I grumble as I crawl to the edge of the bed. If I missed dinner, I'm going to be pissed, because lunch wasn't something I was provided with before I left the cell.

Justine enters the room, a whistle falling from her lips. "Damn, girl. Already in his bed? I assumed eventually, but not this quickly."

I cut a glare at her as I slide off the mattress. "I wasn't sharing it *with* him." My hand gestures over the now-empty king-size mattress. "Clearly."

Her eyes trail over the disheveled pillows and rumpled blankets before landing back on me. "But I bet you were enjoying his sandalwood scent all around you."

"And here I thought we were going to be friends," I mutter, brushing past her to find a clock in this stupid place.

Justine follows closely behind. "Whatcha doing?"

"Wondering what time it is and if I can still get food," I say just as the aroma of pasta surrounds me. My head whips back toward her. "Is that alfredo?"

She nods but crosses her arms, an evil smirk on her face. "But if we're not friends, I can gladly take back what I brought."

"Don't you fucking dare," I say quickly, my hunger growing increasingly insistent. Stress and food have always been intertwined for me, and the desire to devour every carb in sight is nearly overwhelming.

"Alright, fine," she concedes. "Just know that by eating that food, you're locking yourself into a contract with me. We're going to be friends, and there's no going back on that."

"I wouldn't dream of it." The words fall easily from my lips. I genuinely like Justine. She has a way of making me relax amidst the chaos. She's outspoken, smart, and kind. And if she keeps bringing me food, I might just propose to her.

A part of me knows I shouldn't so easily trust her, but when I look into Justine's hazel eyes, there's a flutter in my chest that calms my raging nerves. There's just something genuine about her that I can't—or more likely don't want to—ignore. I need someone in my corner or I might really lose my shit. She's a gamble I'm willing to take for my sanity.

Sitting at the table, I motion for her to join me, my eyes fixated on the feast before us—fresh breadsticks, chicken alfredo, and a Caesar salad. The combined scents are mouth-watering, overpowering any thoughts of Luca.

"What?" I ask, uncovering the warm goodness and nearly melting in my seat at the sight of the delectable spread.

"Luca asked me to bring you food again," Justine answers, a hint of mischief in her voice. "Do you know why? Of course, you don't. You were sleeping. But he knew that because he came up here to check on you and get you food himself."

My head shakes involuntarily, and I quickly swallow my pasta to avoid choking. "Not possible," I manage to mumble.

Her grin widens, and she meets my gaze head-on. "Oh, my new friend. It absolutely is. Luca Monroe likes you."

I place my fork down, my heart skipping a beat as I laugh incredulously. "You're on crack if you think that. He wants to murder me."

Justine's expression turns serious, her gaze unwavering. "I promise you, Olivia. I have no intention of lying to you. Not for Luca or any other purpose. I told you to comply, because I truly believe it's the easiest and quickest way to get you out of here. But in the few months I've lived in this compound, they have never brought a witness back here. Do you know how I arrived?"

I hesitate before answering. I don't want to know the answer, but she tells me anyway.

"I was being stalked, and Jaxon came to my rescue,"

she reveals. "He basically kidnapped me off the street and brought me here. Then he killed my stalker. I thought this would terrify me, that this was never a life I could live. But they're not evil men, Olivia. They do bad things, but not for fun. They protect what they deem worthy of their fierceness. Luca has deemed you worthy. Him bringing you here is a big deal, even if he's still being an asshole."

I'm at a loss for words, my breath caught in my throat. This can't be true. I don't want to know these things, because ignoring my attraction to the man I consider a monster is already challenging enough. To hear Justine speak of him in this manner...it makes my heart constrict.

This isn't the world for me. I'm glad that Justine has found some semblance of peace here, but it's not a life I can embrace. I've already lost so much, and surrendering my freedom to the mafia is not an option for me. No way in hell. What I long for are the images I drew—the garden in my mother's backyard, the flowers that brought light into my life. More than anything, I need them to honor my mother's memory.

Those thoughts remind me that there are more important matters to discuss than Luca Monroe and what he *isn't* feeling for me.

"Can I ask a big favor of you?" I say to Justine, changing the subject not only to avoid any emotions she might force me to deal with, but because saving the house is at the top of my priority list.

Justine reaches for my hand beside my plate,

squeezing it reassuringly. "You can ask, and I'll do my best to make it happen."

That's the best I can hope for, and I don't resent her for that answer. It's just another reason I can't stay here any longer than necessary.

"When my mother died, she left me her house but also a mountain of bills," I explain, "including past-due property taxes that will soon lead to her house being auctioned if I don't pay. I was supposed to deal with it this week, but that won't happen without help. My friend Tori can handle everything, but she'll start asking questions about my whereabouts. I have an idea of what we could tell her—"

Justine cuts me off with a wave of her hand. "Nonsense. We don't need to involve Tori. These men have money coming out of their ears. Let me handle this. Give me the address, and I'll make all these problems go away for you."

I blink, uncertain how to respond. "I have some money—"

"No," she states firmly. "This is the least we can do for you. Let me handle this. Please."

My mother always told me to never look a gift horse in the mouth. Though, I can't help but wonder if accepting her help will further entangle me with these people. Can I afford that? Absolutely not. But with the unwavering determination in Justine's gaze, I don't feel like I have any other choice.

"Fine, but I'll pay you back when this is all done," I say, picking up my fork again, because I can't fathom letting this meal go cold. Not only because I'm starving but because of Luca's earlier warning about not being wasteful.

Her lips thin. "Yeah, I'll be sure to make sure you do that."

She won't, but that doesn't mean I won't try. It's a matter of principle.

The door to the room swings open, drawing our attention. As Luca walks in, Justine swiftly rises to her feet.

"Enjoy your dinner," she says. "I'll check in on you tomorrow morning."

Hopefully that will be to get my address and make sure my mother's house isn't sold out from under me.

As she leaves, she nods at Luca. He says nothing to her, barely even giving her a glance. Instead, his eyes seem to be searching the room.

"Did you decide to sleep earlier so you didn't have to be in bed with me tonight?" he asks with a challenging tone once we're alone.

Oh, this royal pain in my ass.

"I slept because some psycho kept me in a cold cell for two days and I was exhausted," I snap back. Apparently, playing coy isn't going to work for me. I at least gave it a valiant try.

He begins to unbutton his white dress shirt, and my eyes widen. He can't possibly undress right here, in the main living area.

"Keep using that smart mouth of yours as you are and you just might find yourself back there," he warns, continuing to release several more buttons. His shirt begins to open up, revealing a muscular physique with a tattoo I can barely make out over his left pec and a smattering of hair over his chest.

Damn it. Everything about this situation is so fucked.

I don't bother to apologize for my attitude and return my attention to my food, which is getting colder by the second. I start shoveling the pasta into my mouth so that I don't have to continue conversing with this man.

He is dangerous for more than one reason, and my story won't be like Justine's.

I sense him walking by the table where I sit, and he says nothing more, continuing to the bedroom. My eyes betray me, glancing up as he passes, and I can't help but check out his backside.

His shirt is all the way off now, held by one hand at his side. I let my gaze travel slowly over his naked broad shoulders, down his back, noticing a couple of scars that look a lot like bullet wounds.

That has my lips turning down and my eyes focusing back on my food.

I remind myself that this is not the man or the life for me. I've just been through the traumatic experience of losing my mother then being kidnapped by a man who also saved my life. As soon as I can escape from this place, I have no doubt that any flicker of attraction I feel now will fade away effortlessly.

It has to.

11

LUCA

Inviting this woman into my personal space had seemed like a logical solution earlier, but now that she's here, the absurdity of it all weighs heavily on me. Seeing her cleaned up, her presence in my bed... It tempts me to banish her back to the cell.

Yet, I made this choice against the advice of others. Unless Olivia does something to warrant being thrown back into that cage, I won't prove them right. I won't let them know how deeply she bothers me.

Instead, I'm going to have to think more strategically. Find a way to finish this mess with Titan and get Olivia out of my life for good. All sooner rather than later.

I shower for the second time that day just to give me something to do, and once I step back into the bedroom, she still hasn't returned. One glance through the door shows me she's not at the table, either.

With only a towel wrapped around my waist, I look

out into the living room and find her with the paper and pencil I found shoved under her pillow back in the cell.

She'd been sketching flowers, quite well in fact. When I had the items that Justine had given her brought up, I'd purposely left the paper out where she'd easily find it.

I might be a murderer, but I'm not a monster. I haven't forgotten that this woman just lost her mother, been shot at, and was essentially kidnapped.

While this is currently the safest place for her—something she's yet to realize—and I don't feel bad about holding her against her will, I also need her to cooperate if things are going to be settled quickly.

Giving her what I can to bring some solace isn't me being soft. It's me knowing how best to get what I want. That's what I keep telling myself each time I do something that benefits this woman more than it does me. At least, for the moment.

I go back to my room and put on black sweatpants, dry my hair with a towel once more before heading out to the living room, and head to the small fridge behind the bar for a bottle of water. As I twist the cap off, I turn to Olivia.

Her gaze flicks up toward me, and her pencil halts its movement over the page. Her flushed cheeks and the faint scraping of her teeth over her luscious lips catch my attention.

Fuck, why couldn't she be an old hag?

Finishing the water, I approach her. "Are you planning to stay out here?"

Her gaze cautiously meets mine. "Would that be preferable for you?"

"What would have been preferable for me is if you had left the hotel through the front, like any normal fucking person," I practically growl.

She swallows nervously. "Right. Well, that didn't happen."

"Clearly." My chest expands, and I don't miss how her eyes observe the action. "You can sleep wherever you want, but if you're sleeping in my bed, then you better be in there soon. I don't take being woken up well."

She nearly snorts. "I'm not sure you take anything *well*."

Leaning forward, I place my hands on the cushion behind her, boxing her in. "Oh, I do. As long as I get what I want. And if you haven't realized this yet, Little Raven, I always do."

Her mouth parts as I inch closer, but I don't do what she expects. I don't own her lips like my mouth wants to. I jerk away and, without turning back, go into my bedroom. Once she can no longer see me, I remind her of one thing. "Remember, if you wake me up, that cage you were in will feel like a five-star hotel."

She says nothing in return, which takes me by surprise, given how freely she spoke before, but I don't let that stop me from resuming my nightly routine. All except one thing.

Normally, I'd wear nothing to bed, but knowing there's a chance Olivia will be in my bed and that I need to maintain control in this situation, I know better than to be naked with her in arm's reach.

With the way she responds to me, neither of us need that temptation.

This woman needs to remain exactly what she is: a witness and someone to be used to keep Titan from further irritating me.

I haven't been able to forget what Jax said earlier about the possibility of Titan killing Senator McAdams just to fuck with my business.

Part of me would like to believe the senator's death resulted from his greed, attempting to profit from multiple mafia groups. However, regardless of how easy the man was to manipulate and blackmail, he never acted stupidly in his dealings with me. That alone gives Jax's assumption some weight, along with other pieces I've been putting together throughout the day.

Titan Moretti has been cautious in his moves, but he's finally been caught. He'll now face the choice of disappearing or dying by my hand. While the latter would assure he's never a problem again, his death would also ignite a war in our world that I'd rather avoid.

I prefer my position in the business world to that of a mafia king. Nevertheless, I won't shy away from a fight. I'll eliminate him without hesitation if I think for one second that he's not amicable to my proposition. Protecting the empire that I've built is what matters most to me. I've transformed an underground enterprise into a thriving multibillion-dollar business, one that's reputable.

That doesn't mean I'll ever fully distance myself from

the darker side of my business. There's a part of me that finds release in knowing what I'm capable of. Yet, I've fought to ensure I don't have to involve myself further with individuals like Titan since my father's murder. He believed that expanding mafia connections would bring protection, but it's ultimately what cost him his life. I made sure to learn from that before I found myself with the same fate.

I lay in bed, staring at the cream-colored ceiling with my hands tucked behind my head, trying to cease the rampant thoughts I've allowed to enter my mind.

Counting down from one hundred typically does the trick, but with Olivia's floral scent embedded into the pillows around me, I'm ready to head downstairs and use the gym.

Before I can swing my legs off the bed, the audacious woman enters the bedroom with her head held high. Even in the dim lighting, I can see her eyes fixed on me. I say nothing as she approaches, standing beside the bed in silence. For several moments, only the whirring of the ceiling fan fills the room.

Then, she starts rearranging the pillows. "What are you doing?" I demand.

"You said the bedding wasn't allowed on the floor," she replies. "But you didn't say it couldn't be moved around."

When she finishes, a wall of pillows stands between us, and she places one last pillow at the foot of the bed before lifting the comforter and climbing in.

"Don't blame me if you end up with a foot in your

face tonight," I state. "I'm used to having the bed to myself. I move around. A lot."

This seems to give her pause, but she stays resolute in her decision and gives me her back. "I'll just keep my face this way."

"Suit yourself."

"I will."

Her retort makes my fingers tighten into fists as I force myself to close my eyes, resume counting, and consider that maybe a confrontation with Titan Moretti wouldn't be so bad. The sooner he's neutralized, the sooner Olivia will be out of my bed and out of my system.

I may desire her, but I won't indulge in her—not now, not ever. I wasn't lying earlier when I said I always get what I want, but I also know when taking what I want puts everything else I deem important at risk. My world is not meant for her. I knew that the moment I saw her wide blue eyes on that stage, meaning...Olivia Danes is the one thing I'll deny myself.

———

THE NEXT MORNING, I GET INTO THE SUV ON MY way to work and find Jaxon behind the wheel. While that's not abnormal, the pensive look on his face is. He's not usually one to hold back his thoughts.

"What?" I ask once I'm settled in the back seat and he's driving.

"Justine spoke with Olivia again last night," he says, as if he doesn't know I came home to see that for myself.

"Your point?" I'm rather sure he's aware I asked his girlfriend to bring Olivia food, so I don't know why Jaxon seems so put off by the two women speaking.

"Olivia asked Justine to do her a favor," he adds, keeping his eyes on the road.

Now, this is news to me.

"What sort of favor and how did Justine respond?" I ask calmly.

Jaxon remains quiet as he moves in and out of the traffic before he answers. "The boxes Damon had to sort through when he retrieved some of Olivia's things weren't because she had just moved in. She was moving out and into her mother's house. At least between what Olivia said and the texts with Tori, that's what Justine put together."

I raise a brow, not seeing his point. "What's the problem? Or even the favor? Does Olivia need her belongings moved?"

While not something any of my men normally do, it's not the oddest thing to request.

He shakes his head. "Her mom wasn't keeping up with the bills. Olivia needs some debts to be paid or she's going to lose the house her mother left her."

Again, I'm taken aback that Olivia hasn't used her title as witness to get more things that she needs. She's merely put up with my treatment. Well, along with having an attitude and not a proper amount of fear for the situation she's in.

She could have bargained: her compliance for her mother's home.

Yet, it's almost as if so much shit has been thrown at her recently that she doesn't care if she lives or dies.

The thought tastes sour to me.

"Justine told me she's going to pay all the bills for Olivia, even though Olivia says she has money to make some of the payments," Jaxon adds.

My stare moves out the window, and I do something I shouldn't.

"No," I say. "I'll take care of it."

He fights a grin. "I already told her to hold off until I spoke with you."

"This isn't to be shared with Olivia," I demand gruffly. I can't be soft with her. She can't be a weakness in my world.

Still, I know that I need to help her. The reason for it is beyond me. I rarely help anyone who isn't living under the same roof as me, but even as I stare at the passing traffic, I know Olivia Danes isn't just anyone.

Even more, she's a woman I shouldn't claim. Yet... there's a part of me already wondering what she'll think about me taking care of her after what she's already witnessed.

Will she still think of me as a monster, or will she see that I only do what I do to protect what I care most about?

12

OLIVIA

Nine long days have passed since I found myself trapped in this suffocating place. Cut off from the outside world, confined within Luca's home. There have been moments when I've yearned to return to the underground cell, but I've managed to restrain myself each time.

I need my freedom back. Not the feigned one I have by being in Luca's room. I want my life outside of this compound back, and I'm not going to get that by being sequestered in the darkness.

The last seven days since exiting the underground cage have blurred together, each one an eerie reflection of the other. I wake up alone in Luca's bed, go through the motions of showering, dressing, and waiting for Justine. She brings me breakfast and any updates she can gather, along with continued requests for ways to placate Tori who continues to reach out daily, wondering where the hell I've disappeared to. As much as I wish to find a way to tell her the truth, this isn't something I want my best friend wrapped up in.

In the hours I'm alone in the apartment, I fill them by drawing, reading, or rewatching episodes of *Friends* until the next meal arrives.

It's not always Justine who visits any more. Sometimes it's Jaxon, and a few times it's been Markus, the most elusive member of Luca's group that I've met. He doesn't speak when he enters. Hell, he doesn't even look at me. Just sets the tray of food on the table and exits as quietly as he came.

Evenings prove to be the most challenging. During the day, when Luca isn't taking up all the space in his room with his presence, I can momentarily forget how much my body wants the man I should find repulsive, but at night...

My skin yearns for his touch. My very being pulses in sync with his breath as we sleep side by side, always separated by the fortress of pillows I diligently build each night. We never touch, but the magnetic force between us feels palpable.

He never returns before nine, and we're in bed by ten. Our short hour together is typically spent in silence. Most questions I ask he refuses to answer, and no matter if I'm polite or rude, he remains indifferent...until I find his eyes on me.

When he's staring, that's when I feel weakest. As if this man could demand anything of me and my resistance to him would be futile.

The darkness within him has grown on me, no matter

how much I try to fight it. I can hardly breathe when he's near, and sleeping without touching him or even myself becomes harder every passing night. Hell, I've even started stashing pillows under the bed so there aren't as many to place between us.

Yes, I'm well aware of my own madness, lusting after my captor. But damn it, he's too fucking enigmatic to resist.

The only good things I've managed to experience this last week have been getting lost in my art and having Justine tell me that my mother's house isn't at risk any longer. She was vague on the details, but I attributed that to her not wanting me to continue insisting that I pay them back. Still, I'm just glad it's one less thing I need to worry about for now. Even more so, she took care of making sure all of the items at my apartment were moved over to the house before they got trashed by my landlord when my move-out day arrived.

Letting all of the things be done for me and not having any control is hard to accept, but I get a little better at it with each passing day.

At precisely nine o'clock, the lock disengages on the steel door, and Luca strolls into the room, hands casually tucked into his pockets, a grin gracing his lips. I briefly close my eyes and curse the cruel fate that would make this man even more irresistible with a simple smile. It shouldn't be possible, but it is, and I avert my gaze, unwilling to succumb to his charm as he heads to his personal bar in the living room to pour himself a drink.

"Want anything?" he asks, taking me by surprise.

Not once in the last week has he offered to do anything for me. Justine tries to convince me that Luca wants me, but I've had no proof of that except for those brief moments when he stares at me. His eyes darken, his jaw tightens, and sometimes I swear I even hear a rumble in his chest.

Though, I'm not sure if those are signs of a desire to have me or kill me.

"No, thanks," I finally answer, then give my attention back to the paper in front of me. I got my paints from Justine, but sketching has seemed safer...less messy.

Luca's shadow looms over me, but I don't look up. That also seems *safer*. Only, he doesn't go away like I expect.

"I'm going out tonight," he states, a glass of whiskey in one hand and the other settled back into the pocket of his black slacks.

"I won't wait up, don't worry," I reply, doing my best to keep my gaze from flicking too far up while I ignore the pang of jealousy that flits through me. What the fuck is wrong with me? I shouldn't care if he's going out, likely to be hit on by other women, maybe even touched by them...

This man is not mine, and he never will be.

He bends down, taking my pad of paper and tossing it onto the slate coffee table beside him. "Get dressed."

I finally meet his stare head on and steel myself for the power this man seems to have over me. "Excuse me?"

"You're going with us," he says, as if this is something normal. "Justine will be there, and I need all of the men I trust closest with me, meaning you can't be left here alone."

"Why?" I ask, my uncertainty encompassing both aspects of his statement.

He glowers down at me where I've stayed on the couch. "Have you not grasped that there are people who would rather you cease breathing?"

"Oh, I have," I retort, my voice filled with a mixture of defiance and suspicion. "A few of them likely even sleep under this roof."

Silence stretches between us, and Luca offers no response. "Get dressed, Raven. I won't ask again," he commands before disappearing into his bedroom.

I don't want to go. I don't want to be around more of his people. Yet, this might be an opportunity for me to escape. Sure, people want me dead, but I'm not stupid. If I could get away, I wouldn't go home. I'd run to... Hell, I don't know, but anything has to be better than here with...this man.

Though, as my eyes catch the flowers that I was drawing only a few minutes before, my chest constricts at the thought of leaving everything behind. Never having anything of my mother's to physically remember her by. Never planting the garden my thoughts have become so obsessed with since my capture.

Can I really give all that up to stay alive on my own terms? That's a question I don't actually have an answer to.

Luca might be the devil reincarnate, but he has kept his word so far. Maybe it's a question I don't have to answer. With how giddy he seemed walking into the room tonight, maybe this will all be over sooner rather than later.

Just as I stand to go into the bedroom to change, Luca steps out of the room as if he's going to reprimand me for not doing as he commanded. A shiver moves down my spine and settles at my core, wondering just how he might do that.

Mother fuck. I need to get out of this place.

"Is there a dress code for where we're going?" I ask, moving past him, careful not to brush against his chest as I do.

He's silent for another beat, then says, "I'll have Justine bring you some dresses."

Luca retrieves his phone from the bed and heads toward his closet. I don't linger to watch him change; the torment of witnessing such a spectacle is one I don't need to endure. Instead, I make my way to the bathroom, releasing my hair from the ponytail it has been trapped in all day. With the straightener I discovered amongst my belongings, I tame my hair, giving it soft waves.

As I sweep mascara onto my lashes, I hear a faint knock at the door. Luca's heavy footsteps echo through the room, but I remain in the bathroom, avoiding the front door I've learned is equipped to keep me contained. There's no reason to touch it now.

Justine appears in my peripheral vision, and I turn my head to find her wearing a wicked grin, her hands silently clapping with excitement. "We're going out!"

Her words are almost a whisper, but the anticipation radiates from her.

"I'm only going because Luca doesn't trust me to be left alone in the compound," I reply, not sharing in her enthusiasm.

She grabs my wrist and pulls me out of the bathroom. "Whatever, Debby Downer. Choose one." Justine points at the dresses she's tossed on the bed, then places her hand over a maroon dress. "This would look stunning on you."

I consider her suggestion, knowing she's not entirely wrong, but my eyes are drawn to the green satin dress next to it. "What about this one?"

"Oh, that's my second favorite," she exclaims. "As long as you didn't pick the black one, I'm happy."

I chuckle. "Then why did you bring it?"

"Because you're allowed to make your own choices with me, and since you wore that black dress for the auction, I wanted to make sure you had all the options available that you might want."

Ah, the black sequin number that I've yet to see since getting some of my things back. I've tried not to think too much about that over the last week.

I grab the green dress and step into the bathroom. As I start to close the door, Justine shakes her head. "I didn't take you for a prude."

"If it was only you in this apartment, I wouldn't be," I say, knowing that getting naked in front of Luca is the last thing anyone needs. Most of all, me.

He hasn't come back into the bedroom since Justine

arrived, but I still don't take the chance and close the bathroom door instead.

With a mixture of apprehension and a faint glimmer of hope, I strip down to my underwear and step into the dress, relishing the feeling of the smooth emerald fabric against my skin. The dress clings to my curves, accentuating them in a way that makes me feel both vulnerable and powerful. It's as if the dress was tailored to fit me perfectly, enhancing my confidence.

As I zip up the dress with some effort, my fingers lingering on the delicate fabric, I catch my reflection in the mirror. The simplicity of the design belies its allure. The sharp V-neckline plunges down, hinting at a sultry elegance, while the absence of embellishments allows the satin to speak for itself.

With one more check of my hair, I gather my courage and open the bathroom door, accepting that I'm allowed to be at least a little excited to get out of this apartment prison. It's been too many days since I've properly seen sunshine and, even though it's late evening now, the eagerness to stand under the night sky grows with every passing second since putting on the dress.

To my surprise, when I walk out of the bathroom, Justine and Luca are locked in a confrontation. They turn toward me as I enter, their gazes clashing for a moment before Luca abruptly exits the bedroom, leaving me standing there, a mix of emotions swirling within me.

"Damn, girl," Justine says, her voice filled with admiration as she whistles appreciatively. "You're like fucking fire in that dress."

A blush creeps onto my cheeks, but beneath the surface, there's a tightness in my chest. I had hoped for some kind of acknowledgement from Luca, but his dismissal cuts deeper than I care to admit, especially after the positive mood he came home in.

Justine tosses black heels onto the bed. "Put those on and then let's go. We can't be late."

"What is it that we're even doing?" I ask as I grab the shoes and lean against the mattress.

"Can't say, but we'll be enjoying ourselves while the men attend to business." Her words fill me with frustration, slashing away at my previous thrill, but maybe it's better this way.

The less I know, the less of a threat I am.

She loops her arm through mine once I'm ready, and we walk out into the living room together. Luca is standing there, joined by Jaxon who lights up when he sees Justine. A grin tugs at the side of his mouth, and his eyes darken while he drinks her in.

I try to pull away, feeling as if I'm intruding on a private moment, but Justine's grip on me doesn't loosen.

"Let's go," Luca's gruff voice announces, then gone is the man who told me to get dressed earlier.

I'm not sure if it's me or something Justine said to change his demeanor, but I decide I don't care. I can't control his emotions, just like I can't control my staying in this house. All I can do is make sure that I do my best to enjoy seeing the outside world after more than a week of captivity, even if it's brief.

Leaving the room behind, I take in the small landing

outside Luca's door. The absence of windows and personal touches accentuates the sterile atmosphere, reminding me of the darkness that lurks within these walls. Cream-colored walls and dark wood floors, seemingly innocuous but bearing the weight of untold stories and hidden secrets.

The elevator opens, and we all step in. Jaxon pulls Justine into his embrace, not hiding even an ounce of his affection for my new friend. A pang of jealousy fills me. Not because I want Luca to be doing the same thing to me, but because nobody has ever looked at me like Jaxon does her. With a passion so fierce that he'd let the world burn before losing her.

Luca is the first to step out when we get to the garage. He heads toward the SUV that brought me here, and standing next to the doors are two of the few men I've met since staying here: Markus and Damon.

Markus is the silent type that terrifies me more than anyone else I've seen since arriving at the compound. His eyes so brown that they're nearly black are always pinched at the sides, as if he's in constant pain, and the tattoos made of dark imagery that I've seen on his arms don't help my imagination from assuming the worst about him.

Damon is a lighter version of Markus and looks younger than the rest of these men, likely in his twenties. He has blond hair that's longer on top and sweeps to the side but doesn't go past his neck. His eyes are light blue, and I can't see any visible marks on him. He's also only made an appearance in Luca's room once, but I don't for one second assume this man is any more innocent than the others.

Dressed in black slacks, white dress shirts, and suitcoats left casually open, the four men exude an air of controlled power, masking their true nature beneath a veneer of sophistication. It's a chilling reminder of the dangers that surround me.

Markus gets into the driver's seat, Damon takes the passenger, while Justine and Jaxon get into the last row, meaning I'm stuck in the middle with Luca. Just like when I'd last been in here with him, I press myself as close as I can get to the door and stare out of the window.

The SUV fills with a tense silence, and I close my eyes briefly, praying that whatever we're headed out to accomplish won't further shatter my already fragile existence in this unknown world.

13

OLIVIA

As we're ushered through a discreet back door, the feeling of Luca's firm grip on my bicep as he leads the way up a set of stairs just inside the pulsating nightclub is a reminder this isn't a *fun* outing. Soft blue and purple lights bathe the open space, casting an ethereal glow upon white couches and tables filled with lively patrons. The steady beat of music reverberates through the air, creating an atmosphere of vibrant energy that I can't seem to connect with.

Ascending to the second level, my eyes catch sight of several private rooms with tinted glass windows, shielding the interiors from prying eyes. We make our way to the third room, accompanied only by Jaxon and Justine. As the door closes behind us, a profound silence envelops the area, causing me to reflexively open my mouth, attempting to alleviate the pressure in my ears from the sudden change in noise.

Luca firmly pushes me toward the wrap-around

couch, his voice laden with authority. "Stay there. You're not to leave this room or open that door for any reason. Do you understand me?"

Raising an eyebrow, I question his decision. "You're leaving me here alone?"

"No, Justine will be with you," he replies, his gaze shifting to her with a lethal intensity. "And she knows what's at stake if you leave."

"I've got your girl, Luc," Justine chimes in, striding away from Jaxon and settling next to me on the couch. "We'll order some food and drinks and be just fine right here."

Nobody corrects her use of "your girl," and though I'm tempted to, I opt to remain silent. In this moment, being away from Luca's watchful gaze takes precedence over making a needless point.

The door swings open, revealing Damon peering in. "They're ready."

Luca points at me and then at Justine, his voice seething with urgency. "Stay fucking put. Someone will be outside the door at all times."

Justine blows a kiss to Jaxon, who returns it with a wink, before diverting her attention to me. "What do you want to drink?" She picks up a tablet from the table near the couch, her fingers deftly navigating the options. "They have the best fried calamari here, too."

"I'll have whatever you're having," I absentmindedly reply. The excitement I anticipated would come from being outside the compound fails to materialize. Instead, my stomach churns with unease, and the silence of the room feels suffocating.

My fingers twist together as I glance around the private area. I can see out the window, but without standing, all I see are the lights hanging from the ceiling. To my right is a curtain and another door half hidden behind it.

"Where does that go?" I ask with a nod.

Justine glances around me. "Service area. They'll bring our food through there." Her fingers continue flicking through the screens and adding items to our order effortlessly, as if she's been here a dozen times before. "Alright, one order of fried calamari, two Apple Fuckers to get us started, and two Leg Spreaders to knock us on our asses."

I tilt my head and blink. "What the fuck did you just say?"

She laughs, her auburn hair cascading behind her. "Just go with it. We're celebrating your freedom tonight."

"Freedom?" I echo, my skepticism evident. "Sitting in a room I can't leave that I'm sure has a guard outside the door doesn't spell freedom to me."

Undeterred, she finalizes the order and sets the tablet down. "This is the first step, my friend. Just you wait and see."

I mean, it's not as if I have any other choice, and her continued confidence is rubbing off on me, brightening my mood and finally relaxing my shoulders. "So, what now?"

The door opens on my right, and I nearly piss myself.

Apparently, I'm taking the perceived threats to my life more seriously than I realized.

Thankfully, there isn't a deranged member of the mafia walking into the room. Only a waiter, carrying a tray of four drinks.

"Ladies." He bows lightly, then sets the alcohol in front of us. "Your food will be up shortly. Enjoy."

I eye the green-colored shot and yellowish cocktail. "Do I want to know what's in these?"

Justine offers me one of her signature devious grins. "Nope." She reaches for both shots, hands me one, then clinks hers against mine. "Bottoms up!"

I hesitate only for a second, then follow her movements. *Fuck it*, I think. She's right. I need to enjoy this modicum of freedom. At least it's a change in scenery.

An explosion of tangy Vodka hits my tongue, then burns down my throat. I pinch my eyes closed and swallow quickly, doing my best not to gag. Hard alcohol has never been my preference, but I'm hanging out with the mafia. Trying new things seems like something I shouldn't say no to.

"Delicious, right?" Justine wipes a trace of the drink from the corner of her mouth. "The Leg Spreader is even better."

As we simultaneously reach for our drinks, our hands collide, causing one of the martini glasses to teeter over the edge of the table and spill onto Justine's legs, soaking one of her shoes.

Gasping, I instinctively cover my mouth with both hands. "I'm so sorry."

She laughs, gesturing for me to calm down. "All good. I'll just pop into the ladies' room real quick." Her expression turns serious. "Please don't leave."

I hold up three fingers. "I wouldn't dream of it."

The words fall easily from my lips. Even though I despise my captivity, I can acknowledge that Luca has in fact kept me safe. And Justine's belief in the threat against me reinforces the knowledge that until the people who wish me dead are...dealt with, I won't be going anywhere. No matter how much I often wish otherwise.

As I grab the tablet to order Justine another drink, assuming it can't be that hard, I realize this is the first time I've truly come to accept my situation. I thought I would feel an overwhelming sense of loss by admitting I have no control over my life. Instead, there's a dose of relief that fills me that I no longer have to fight everything being forced on me.

Justine is already out the door, and it takes me more than a minute to find Leg Spreader on the menu. When I see the four different types of liquor included in the ingredients, I cringe. The toilet might be my pillow tonight if I let Justine continue to be the picker of drinks.

I've barely set the tablet down when the curtain moves, but nobody enters the room. My stomach drops as if I've just jumped off the highest cliff. "Hello?" I say, then add, "Luca?"

A little name-drop never hurt anyone. *Right?*

"Luca's preoccupied, but don't worry, I'm here to

make sure you're taken care of," a raspy voice emerges from the shadows, sending a shiver down my spine. The dim lighting of the room makes it difficult to discern the figure, heightening my sense of vulnerability.

My mind races, considering my options. The pulsating music I know is outside the room drowns out any potential screams for help. I glance at the door, my heart pounding, contemplating the possibility of escape. I'm not sure I'll be quick, but a surge of adrenaline propels me forward with a shred of hope as I make a dash for the exit only a second later.

Just as I reach out, hoping for safety from whoever this stranger is, a powerful force collides with me, sending me sprawling to the ground. Pain shoots through my face as it connects with the hard tile, leaving me disoriented and helpless, just inches away from the door.

My legs flail out in a desperate attempt to free myself, but strong fingers grip my hair, yanking me to the side. The man's weight presses me down, immobilizing me completely. Panic courses through my veins, unsure what the hell I'm supposed to do now.

"Luca Monroe is going to kill you," I spit out defiantly, though the words hold a touch of uncertainty. I have no idea if Luca holds that much power to harm whoever this is, but I grasp at any hope of deterring this fucker.

He laughs, his eyes wrinkling at the corners, and revealing a gap between his teeth. "He could if he knew who I was, but little Luca won't find me, sweetheart. I've been at this game a lot longer than he has."

His words make my heart sink as I scrutinize his features, committing every detail to memory. I don't know what he intends to do with me, but if I survive whatever is about to happen, then I can at least tell Luca everything possible.

His older age is apparent, with dark hair heavily peppered with grey strands. His brown eyes hold a ring of amber, adding a sinister glimmer to his gaze. A lump protrudes over the bridge of his nose, likely a remnant of past encounters. He's wearing a black long-sleeve shirt with jeans that I can't exactly tell the color of from my pinned position.

His open palm strikes my already sore cheek, the pain reverberating through my face. "Don't fucking look at me like that."

I refuse to look away, meeting his gaze head-on. But my defiance only seems to fuel his sadistic pleasure.

Forcibly flipped onto my stomach, my view of him and the room is snatched away. Helplessness washes over me, but a surge of determination swiftly replaces it once I realize that my hands are momentarily free. I start to push myself out from underneath him, but cool metal presses against my neck.

"Don't fucking move," he hisses. "We wouldn't want to make a mess, would we?"

Fear takes hold, but I refuse to let it paralyze me. The blade drags across my shoulder, leaving a stinging sensation, a mark that will undoubtedly remind me of this moment. Yet, he stops short of drawing blood.

The blade slides under the right strap of my dress

before pulling upward, cutting easily through the satin, but missing my bra as he continues cutting just a few layers into my skin.

"Shall we figure out how many cuts it will take to remove this dress from your body?" he taunts, the excitement in his voice making bile rise in my throat. The true intent behind his words chills me to the core.

Though, time should be on my side. Justine was only going to the bathroom. If I can just keep fighting, I might come out of this relatively unscathed. Yet, something tells me that this man didn't just get lucky with his timing. He most likely waited for the perfect time and probably isn't working alone.

Fuck. Is Justine even okay? She should have been back by now...

A surge of anger surges within me, overriding the fear that begs to consume my entire being. Without hesitating further, I act instinctively, catching him off guard. Thanks to a sudden burst of adrenaline, I force myself up and take my attacker by surprise, sending him sprawling to the side.

My body trembles with exertion as I scramble to my feet, reaching for the drink tray from the table nearest to me.

With both hands gripping the hard plastic, I swing it toward his head, connecting with a satisfying thud. It clips his forehead, drawing blood, but he remains standing, his snarl deepening. "You're going to pay for that, bitch."

His unfiltered rage only serves to fuel my desire to

survive. Before he gets close enough to grab me, I snag the overturned martini glass and smash it over his shoulder, then move to stab him in the neck with the jagged stem.

"Nobody told me you were a fighter," he growls, blocking the glass with his forearm. "And here I was going to go easy on you." He reaches a hand between us and through my legs until he's gripping my underwear and tugging until the weak fabric gives way. "Now, I'm going to make sure you can't ever forget me."

A scream rips from my throat, deep and guttural, as I try to stab him again, but he catches my wrist in his vice-like grip, twisting it mercilessly until I'm forced to release my improvised weapon.

Pain radiates through my body as his knee strikes my stomach, knocking the wind out of me and propelling me backward onto the couch. My head collides with the wall behind me, and for a moment, my vision blurs. But I refuse to surrender to the darkness, fighting to stay conscious. This fucker isn't going to touch me again without a fight every step of the damn way.

My foot lashes out in a last-ditch effort to fend him off. However, he easily evades the blow, his focus solely on his own desires. He unfastens his pants, his intentions sickeningly clear. "I'm going to enjoy this," he hisses, a malicious glint in his eyes.

Sick fucker should be castrated.

Using my fingernails, I claw at his face, leaving trails of crimson across his chin. "Good fucking luck enjoying anything," I seethe, my voice filled with venom.

He retaliates, capturing my wrist once more and

twisting it with brutal force until I'm forced to stop fighting or risk breaking a bone or two. Even as fear and pain threaten to consume and he comes closer, I refuse to give up. I have to keep fighting.

The bastard's face is close enough to mine that his smoky breath fans over my face, making my stomach churn violently as he threatens me. "Touch me again like that and my dick will be the least of your worries, sweetheart."

He raises an arm, likely to strike me again, but what I assume to be his phone in his front pocket vibrates just once and he mutters a curse under his breath.

His fingers grasp my chin, and he crashes his lips onto mine in a forceful, violating kiss. The taste of his vile presence lingers, marking me in a different way. "I'll be seeing you soon, Olivia Danes."

With a final threat hanging in the air, he retreats into the shadows, vanishing through the server's door.

My body convulses, the aftermath of the ordeal threatening to consume me as any adrenaline I'd been pulling from escapes from every limb of my body. I can't contain the tremors that take over. Not even when the main door slams into the wall and shouts enter the otherwise silent room.

"Olivia." My name is more of a growl coming from Luca as his gaze searches the room before landing on me, battered and broken.

I don't move. Hell, I can hardly breathe. When he stalks toward me, I shrink back, afraid of his wrath.

Afraid that he's going to blame me for whatever the fuck just happened...or almost happened.

His hand comes up, and I squeeze my eyes closed. "I'm sorry," I say, tasting the saltiness from the tears I didn't realize are sluicing down my cheeks.

"Justine," Luca's voice cuts through the air, his tone distant. "Get her out of here."

I open my eyes to see Luca's retreating back and a frantic Justine brushing past him, racing for me. "I'm so fucking sorry, Olivia."

Her words unleash a torrent of emotions within me, and I curl inward, wrapping myself in the harsh reality that now engulfs my world.

I've seen a dead senator. Been shot at and kidnapped. People want me dead. And now...someone just came dangerously close to violating me in one of the worst ways possible.

I'm not safe.

Not with Luca. Not anywhere.

14

LUCA

My entire being is a pit of rage that I don't know how to control. Olivia was mine to protect. Mine to keep safe. Mine to command. All fucking mine.

And I failed.

I couldn't even offer her some semblance of comfort without her flinching away from me on that couch, all because I fucked up.

I took her from the one place I knew she would be safe, all because I'm a selfish bastard and wanted her to remain close while I claimed my victory over Titan Moretti.

Someone touched her. Marred her precious face. Put their hands where they weren't welcome.

And that someone is going to fucking die.

It doesn't matter that it's been a full twenty-four hours since everything went to shit at the nightclub and I still don't have hands on the man I now know to be named Abel—an old acquaintance of my father's. He thinks he can hide from me, but he can only stay safe for so long.

Now that I have his name, it's only a matter of time before one of the many leads we've received goes in our favor.

Until then, I've kept my distance from Olivia and will continue to do so. I can't stand the thought of facing her, only to tell her the sick fuck who touched her is still breathing.

It's not right, and I'm going to fucking fix this.

I'm going to find Abel and make him beg for death by the time I'm done with his worthless body.

That's a promise I know I can keep.

———

Too many hours have passed while I've hunted for Abel, but his time has finally run out. We're on our way to get him now, and the thrill I feel at knowing the fucker will soon be locked in my basement is the reason I'll never give up this part of my life.

No matter how well-off I am, or that I could never work another day in my life and be just fine, the high that's floating through my body now is irreplaceable.

The calm at knowing my fists will break Abel's face beyond recognition soon. The joy at anticipating the blood he'll shed. The eagerness to hear his screams echo within the walls that they'll never leave.

None of that can be replaced, and I don't want it to be. This is who I am, and I have no regrets about that.

"We're here," Jaxon announces, his fingers tightening over the steering wheel. He's been just as furious as me over the whole situation, given Justine had been locked in the bathroom and he'd ignored her calls for help since we were meeting with Titan.

The meeting went to shit just as soon as we sat down. Titan pretended that he was ready to back off and wanted to finalize any lingering agreements in person. I have no idea how he knew I was going to bring Olivia with me or how she might end up alone, but by the time we realized he was double-crossing us, it was too late.

He'd disappeared, and Olivia had already been hurt.

I can't think about that now, though. Abel is inside the bar in front of us, and I'm going to drag him out of there myself. I didn't even mind driving nearly three hours to the outskirts of Seattle to do so myself.

I'm out of the SUV within seconds of parking and marching toward the door with Jaxon and Damon right behind me. My palm slams onto the already cracked wooden door, forcing it open hard enough that it crashes against the wall.

All eyes turn toward us, but I'm only concerned with one pair. The one that goes wide.

Abel drops the beer that's at his lips and starts to run, but he doesn't get far. I close the distance between us, ignoring my surroundings as I shove him to the ground.

He blinks rapidly and tries to speak, but I don't give him the opportunity. My fist connects with his face, and he's out cold.

I grab the back of his shirt and start to drag him out the

door. Next to me, Jaxon throws a few hundred-dollar bills on the bar top. "Enjoy a few rounds on us as an apology for interrupting your evening, ladies and gentlemen."

Cheers erupt as we walk out the door without a single problem.

Damon moves ahead of me and opens the back of the SUV, grabbing a syringe already filled with a concoction of ketamine.

Callously, I toss Abel into the trunk and Damon steps up to dose him before tying his arms and legs together. "This should keep him unconscious for four or five hours, but I have another dose in case he wakes up early."

I hold my hand out. "I'll take it and gladly stab him if he does while we're driving."

Damon smirks and shakes his head, but hands over the second syringe.

We get back into the SUV, and it's only a matter of minutes before we're getting back on the interstate and heading South.

I smile nearly the entire time, knowing that soon I'll have my hands on this fucker. As soon as he's been dealt with, Titan Moretti will move back to priority number one for me.

———

Back at the house, we've already moved Abel to the basement and tied him to a chair. A half-dozen buckets of water later, he's finally waking up.

I roll the sleeves of my grey dress shirt up and step toward him, grinning as he snarls at me as if he has any chance of getting out of here alive.

"I'm going to fucking kill you," he says with a shake of his head, attempting to clear the water still dripping down his forehead.

I lean forward and grab his neck tight enough that I know there are going to be bruises on his skin within minutes. "No, you're not. You're going to die right here in this chair, and you know why? Because I'm not my father, Abel. You might have double-crossed him all those years ago and thought you got away with it, but now you're going to pay for not only that, but for touching what's not yours."

"I should have told them to kill you instead of your idiot father," he jeers as if it's supposed to hurt my feelings.

I long ago accepted that my father was dead, and even before that, I'd known he wasn't going to live long. He acted on emotion, but that isn't me. While hurting Abel is personal, I'm also making a point.

Cross my family and you won't survive the consequences.

My fist smashes into his jaw, and bones audibly break as blood and at least one tooth gets spit from Abel's mouth. I turn away from him and go to the table where a selection of knives sits, grabbing the smallest, yet possibly sharpest, one.

I move toward Abel again. His eyes are closed, but

one kick to his shins has him regaining consciousness. "Were you working directly with Titan?"

"Fuck you," he grumbles.

I grab the back of his head and jerk it backward. "Not the answer I'm looking for, Abel. Do you want to make this harder than it needs to be? I'll enjoy that, but I don't think you will."

He remains tight-lipped, and the blade in my hand finds its way into his thigh. "What about now?" I ask over his screeching.

His head thrashes and still no words come out.

Out of frustration, I hit him again, and he passes out once more. I pace a few times in front of him, gaining control of my emotions before I act again.

Jaxon steps forward with another bucket of water, dropping the contents over Abel and waking the idiot back up.

"Let's try this again," I say with absolute calm. "Why were you working with Titan Moretti?"

His head shakes, and I raise the knife again, but he opens his mouth, giving me pause. He starts to talk, except the words are so quiet, I can't hear him.

"Speak up," I demand, but the moment I'm closer to him, he attempts to spit on me.

Narrowly missing the blood splatter, I punch him again, blackening his other eye and growling in frustration.

"He's not going to fucking tell us anything," I seethe.

Jaxon is still in the shadows as he speaks. "Do we really need him to? We know this was Titan."

I do, but I prefer to have things cut and dry when I attack another mafia crew. I want solid proof that he crossed lines he had no business even being near. That way, if any fucker tries to accuse me of acting beyond my reach, I don't have to go to war.

Not that I'm afraid of the fight, but war is wasteful to my men. I'll get what I want in the end, but at a cost I'd rather not pay.

"Wake him up again," I say, knowing I need to show Abel the torture is going to get worse if he doesn't give me what I want.

Jaxon does as I say, and once Abel is coherent, I step closer while holding the knife to his neck. "Since you don't seem to listen well, how about I take your ears next?"

As he shakes his head, I hear a gasp behind us.

"Luca," Olivia says, voice filled with half surprise and half anger. "What the fuck are you doing?"

I could ask her the same damn question.

15

OLIVIA

Darkness envelops me like a steadfast companion. Inside Luca's room, I'm left to my own thoughts, with Justine being my only visitor over the past three days. But even her presence fails to bring me solace, and any sort of joy seems distant.

Despite showering multiple times a day, the stench of my attacker lingers, a constant reminder of the nightmarish ordeal I endured. That along with the wrap around my wrist and red lines marring my skin where the knife cut just enough to taunt me.

The psychopath remains out there, not to mention his threat that he'll return to torment me again. The fear of that weighs heavily on my soul, haunting every waking moment.

That and the fact that Luca abandoned me. He left me in this room, isolated and engulfed by darkness. I lie awake, staring at the ceiling, my heart pounding at every creak and thump in the night.

Sleep is pointless. When I close my eyes, the nightmare repeats itself, only worse because my attacker doesn't get interrupted. He gets his wish to harm me in all the worst ways possible, leaving me damaged enough to beg for death, but I never actually get the sweet relief that dying would bring me.

The longer I remain trapped in this cycle of despair, the more my anger festers. I'm furious about the life I've been forced into, about the uncertainties that plague my mind. I have no way of contacting anyone, no concrete proof that my mother's house hasn't been taken away from me. Justine assures me that everything is fine, that I should focus on my recovery, but she fails to understand that there is no true recovery from something like this. No forgetting the man who attacked me and could reappear at any moment.

I need something, and I hate myself every time Luca's name whispers through my mind. I hate that I wish he was in this room with me, making me promises I have no business asking for.

The fact that he's not yet spoken to me since finding me in that private room makes me wonder things that I know I shouldn't.

However, throughout the last hour, I find myself able to grasp onto the anger that's been overshadowed by the torment for much too long now. Proof that there's still a fire simmering somewhere deep within me that can pull me out of the depths of my nightmares. Its silent fury reminds me that this isn't the end for me. The bastard who violated me won't take my life away. Someday, somehow, and even if it's not the same as before, I can find my peace again.

My hope in the darkness, as Justine would say.

When I found that sentiment so touching during our first meeting, I didn't realize there would be so much fucking darkness.

With newfound determination, I rise from the couch where I have spent endless hours, my eyes fixed on the lifeless television screen. I cast aside the blankets, feeling their weight is no longer comforting but suffocating. I know I can't stay here any longer. I need to break free, to run, to do something that will breathe life back into my shattered existence.

Without a phone, I don't know how I'm going to ask someone to let me out. Then again, I've never actually tried to leave on my own.

A flicker of determination ignites within me. Justine's been coming and going as she pleases. Can I simply walk out the door? I don't know, but I'm damn well going to find out.

Returning to the bedroom, I slip on a pair of shoes, leaving everything else behind. None of it holds any significance anymore. Olivia Danes, the person I used to be, is dead. She no longer exists, not after enduring the horrors of the past two weeks.

As I traverse the living room, my steps quicken with anticipation. There could be someone on the other side of that door, ready to order me back to my confinement. But what if there isn't? What if I've been wasting precious time, believing in the very people who put me in this situation?

My fingers curl tightly around the cold metal handle, my grip tightening as I take a steadying breath. I can do this. I have to do this. I refuse to remain a prisoner, to lose control, to be a victim.

But as I try to force myself to open the door, my body begins to tremble at the thought of being outside, alone. Of that man finding me and following through on his promise to see me "soon."

I squeeze my eyes shut and press my forehead against the steel frame, counting to ten, focusing on each inhale and exhale. In the darkness of my own mind is the weaker version of me, still rocking back and forth on the couch, unable to leave the safety she's found within these walls.

"Fuck!" I scream into the abyss. My fists beat against the door, ignoring the slight pain I still feel in the left one that was twisted harshly at the nightclub.

I don't want to be a prisoner. I don't want to lose control.

My eyes open, and I stare at my now red hands. "I can leave this room. I'm going to leave this room."

Even if I don't escape the compound, I can at least open the door, walk out onto the landing, and see what happens.

I can do this. I have to do this. For me and everything I still want out of this fucked-up thing called life.

My grip tightens on the handle again, and I take another shaky breath, but this time I find the will to twist, to pull the door toward me, and see what's on the other side.

To my surprise, and if I'm honest, a hint of disappointment, there isn't anyone waiting on the other side. No guards to keep me in or to protect me. There is nothing but the waiting elevator.

I hesitate, standing just beyond the threshold of Luca's room, weighing the next step toward my freedom. Ten strides forward and a few buttons to press. That's all it takes. I could go to the kitchen or the garage or anywhere else, just to prove to myself that I haven't been completely broken.

But my insides churn with a mixture of anticipation and dread. Each step feels like a piece of me is being ripped away, leaving me raw and vulnerable. All the while, bile rises in my throat, threatening to spill over if I go one more inch forward.

I want to listen to my body, to stay where I've yet to be harmed, but if I'm being honest with myself, Luca's room is not a sanctuary. It's the place where I've been left to fend for myself, abandoned by the man who plucked me from my old life oh so carelessly.

"Fuck you, Luca Monroe," I seethe into the empty air, a burst of anger mingling with my determination. With newfound resolve, I take that step forward, followed by another and another, until I find myself standing before the elevator, pressing the button to summon it.

I don't know where I'm going, and I doubt I'll venture beyond the confines of this building. But I'm done being the pitiful woman locked away from the world for her own protection. If I'm going to endure this, I need to do something for myself, even if it means only leaving the room to find a friend.

As the elevator arrives, I step inside without hesitation, my gaze fixed on the buttons before me. I have no clue where Justine's room is, so I opt for the first floor, hoping there will be a common area where I might find her more easily.

Justine might try to redirect me back to Luca's room, but it's a risk I'm willing to take. She's claimed to be my friend, and now it's time for her to prove it.

A ding from the elevator makes me jump as it signals my arrival. I wait another second for the doors to part and fold both of my arms over my stomach as if that can keep me together while it feels like I'm falling apart at the seams.

My vision blurs, but I blindly continue forward, reaching a hand in front of me so that I don't run into anything that will cause a commotion.

When my chest tightens too much to breathe, I lean against a wall and stare up at the tall, cream-colored ceiling.

"I can fucking do this," I whisper. Still, I don't know what "this" is, but I'm going to find a destination and get there without losing my damned mind.

As my vision clears, I continue down the hallway, but my progress is halted by the sound of voices echoing from a nearby room. Intrigued, I pause to listen, trying to make out the conversation.

"Did you see Luca toss him down the stairs?" a man's voice carries through the walls. "I'd hate to be the one locked down there with that crazy fucker."

My curiosity is immediately piqued, wondering who the hell they're talking about.

"Good thing it's soundproof down there," another adds, then laughs. "None of us would get any sleep tonight from the torture Luc's undoubtedly going to indulge in."

My gasp is muffled by my hand, and a surge of anger courses through me. Is this why Luca has been avoiding me? Is he out there, hunting people to kill? The realization makes my blood boil.

That motherfucker.

Backtracking the way I came, I get back on the elevator and know exactly where I'm going. My finger jabs so hard at the correct button for the sublevel that I miss and have to press it again. My shoulders rise and fall as my breaths get deeper from my rising fury.

How I could have ever let myself be attracted to this asshole is beyond me, but I can now officially say I hate Luca Monroe with every fiber of my being. He is the worst kind of human in existence and he's about ready to know what I think.

Only the elevator doesn't move. No matter how many times I press the stupid button, the doors don't close. Stupid security. It probably needs a thumbprint, but that can't be the only way down there.

I step back into the hallway and squeeze my eyes closed, thinking hard. There has to be a way to get to the basement. One of the guys mentioned stairs, which gets me thinking. If the power went out, they wouldn't risk being stuck, right?

No, there has to be access somewhere else and I'm going to find it. I go back the way I just came from and continue past the room where the men are. I find myself in another hallway, but the more frustrated I get, the harder my breathing, and with black dots flickering in my vision, I can barely see where I'm going.

I start to open doors, but nothing leads to stairs. I find myself at the kitchen entrance, and I'm tempted to just look for some wine and sit at the counter, but as I give it a solid glance, I see there's another hallway, darker than all the rest, as if it's not used all that often.

"Bring me back a beer, too," I hear someone yell.

That's all it takes to get my feet running toward the darkness. I can't be sent back to my room. Not until I... I don't even fucking know, but I need to see Luca. The "why" can be sorted out later.

I hide in the shadows as I hear the fridge being opened, bottles clinking together, and the rustle of something else. My breath ceases until I hear the sound of retreating footsteps.

Once I'm alone, I start checking more doors. There are only three, and the first one is a storage room with food, but the next one... It's pitch black, and I can't feel any light switches on the wall, but there are stairs.

I could be making a big mistake, but I don't stop myself from stepping forward, holding tight to the railing and making my way down, one careful step at a time.

When I'm at the bottom, a flicker of light shines ahead and I move toward it, shivering in the familiar cold within the stone walls. Now that I'm certain I'm in the right place, my rage returns and I charge forward like a woman scorned.

Technically, Luca never made me any promises, but it was implied in a fucked-up way that he was responsible for keeping me safe. Then, he failed and thinks he can slink off into the shadows without so much as an "I'm sorry I let you down, Raven"?

Fuck. That. Bullshit.

I round another corner of the dank hallways and have to hold my breath. The frigidness in the air and stench penetrating all around me remind me of my first two days here. Still, the emotions that stir within me don't touch the fury I'm clinging to like a lifeline right now.

A long, agonizing groan echoes through the hallway, stopping me in my tracks. My head lowers, and I'm momentarily lost in the darkness, reliving the torment I endured, seeing the image of my shredded dress, battered face, and sprained wrist.

Then, a growl erupts from my throat, snapping me back to reality. I need to confront Luca, to see what could possibly be more important than facing me.

I round the final corner and stand at the entrance of an open area. There's only one light hanging from the center of the ceiling. Beneath it is a man beyond recognition, tied to a metal chair, head lolled forward and passed out until someone from the shadows throws a bucket of water on him, causing him to spit and sputter.

But I don't focus on the broken man for long. My attention is drawn to Luca, standing in front of him. His eyes are dark, filled with an indistinguishable emotion. His sleeves are rolled up as if he attempted to stay clean, but blood splatters still mar the front of him. There are dark circles beneath his eyes, and his jaw is so tense that his cheeks seem hollow beneath several days' worth of hair that's grown since I last saw him.

He holds a knife to the man's neck, leaning closer, menace dripping from his words. "Since you don't seem to listen well, how about I take your ears next?"

The beaten man shakes his head but doesn't speak, and I have to wonder if that's because his jaw is broken based on all the bruises covering his bloodied face.

"Luca," I blurt out without thinking. "What the fuck are you doing?"

His burning gaze slowly shifts toward me, but I'm momentarily distracted by the laughter emanating from the man in the chair. His garbled voice mutters something that sounds disturbingly like, "I told you I'd see you again soon."

Fear engulfs me once again, leaving me paralyzed and unable to act on the revenge I had imagined many times over the last several days. How if I ever saw my attacker again, I would make this man pay for touching me when he had no right to do so.

"Get the fuck out, Olivia." Luca's menacing tone does nothing to snap me out of my stupor.

"You," I whisper.

My attacker tries to speak again, but Luca's fist

crashes into his face, dislodging a tooth or two that clatter onto the cold concrete floor. I can't tear my eyes away from the man bound to the chair. I stand frozen, my mind screaming for action but my body refusing to move.

Luca's imposing form moves to stand before me, his hands gripping my shoulders.

"Leave, Raven," he demands. "Go back to the room and wait for me. Now."

His fingers lift my chin, forcing me to meet his steely gaze. His other hand rests gently on my hip, devoid of the usual roughness I associate with him, and the anger I expected to see on his face is absent.

And just like that, all intentions I had when I came down here, leave me. "Are you going to kill him?" I ask.

Luca nods once, his eyes filled with an unspoken darkness.

"Why?" Confusion clouds my thoughts.

"Because he hurt you."

There's a pause as we both seem to process what he's just admitted.

"And this is who I am," he adds, gently turning me in the other direction, "but it's not who you are. Go back to the room."

He's not wrong about either of those things, yet an unfamiliar part of me stirs deep within. A part I didn't know existed until now. It yearns to stay and witness my attacker's life fade away, to see him suffer just as I have over the past few days. I want to know that the pain I endured has been avenged, if only in a small way.

"Please, Olivia." Luca's voice carries a quiet plea I'd never expect to hear from him. "Just go."

This time, I heed his words. I don't resist. I turn and run, fleeing from the haunting memories, the monster who harmed me, the man I shouldn't care about, and the twisted thoughts that no longer seem so dark.

As if affirming my choice, the elevator I couldn't previously use waits for me, its doors open wide. I step inside and reach back to press the button for the fourth floor, where Luca's room is located. This time, the doors close, promising to seal me off from the grim scene behind, but before they can, I hear the sound of a loud pop reverberating off the concrete walls. My eyes widen, knowing exactly what that sound is. A gunshot.

Did Luca just kill *him*? I'm not sure, and as much as I want to go back and find out, the elevator is already taking me upstairs and I'm certain the button to go back down still won't work for me. Plus, the need to vomit is too strong to push back down.

Rushing past the landing, I forcefully open the steel door that blocks my path, barely making it to the bathroom before I collapse, embracing the toilet.

Bile roughly expels from my stomach, the acidic liquid a reflection of the meager sustenance I've consumed over the past few days. Once I'm done, I realize I need another shower, but this time, I can't be bothered to undress or wait for the water to warm up. I just need to be clean, even though there isn't a speck of dirt on me.

I step under the spray, allowing the cold water to

cascade over me as I lower myself to the tiled floor. Resting my head against the wall at the corner of the shower, I close my eyes. This time, I don't see myself. The image of that bastard tied to the chair graces my thoughts. Only he's not alive any longer. There's a bullet hole in the center of his forehead, and he can't ever hurt another person again.

The steam from the now-warm shower begins to wrap around me, and for the first time in days, I feel tension start to leave my body.

I don't have to be afraid. That man won't come back and find me. I'm going to be okay. He didn't win.

Suddenly, a shadow falls over me, causing me to scream. Any progress I thought I just made is shattered. But then I see Luca standing there, fresh blood staining his face and hands. His dark eyes pierce through me as if he can see into the depths of my soul.

I rise to my feet, unsure of what I'll do, but he steps into the shower with me, staying clothed just like I am.

I reach for his face and brush my thumb over the blood on his cheek. "You killed him."

"I did."

"For me," I add, not as a question, but as a realization. Luca hadn't been ignoring me, I can see that now. He had been hunting—for me.

"He didn't deserve to breathe another day for touching what's...you." His voice falters at the end, leaving me curious about what he truly wanted to say. But I don't push the matter, at least not with words.

My fingers move to the buttons of his ruined dress

shirt, undoing them until he places a hand over mine. "What do you think you're doing?"

"Cleaning up the mess," I say, meeting his intense gaze. "I figure it's the least I can do after thinking you're nothing more than an inconsiderate bastard who left me alone because he couldn't handle a broken woman."

Both of his palms cup my face, holding my cheeks with a tenderness I never imagined him capable of. "There is nothing broken about you, Raven."

As I gaze into his captivating cognac eyes, a part of me wants to believe him, to believe in this moment where all the darkness and pain that has plagued me since meeting him simply melts away.

To believe that I'm just a woman struggling not to fall for the complex man standing before her.

16

LUCA

I expect Olivia to hate me. To despise me for taking her to that club and putting her at risk, allowing that pathetic excuse of a man to put hands on her. I stayed away partly so that I wouldn't be a constant reminder of what happened to her, and also because I couldn't rest until I found who had touched her.

I wasn't even close to done with the torment that bastard deserved when Olivia made her unexpected appearance. At first, she seemed furious about something —I could see it in her eyes—but the moment she recognized Abel, a whirlwind of emotions washed over her.

The fact that I could tell she was torn between wanting to hurt the man who tried to break her and running away was the only reason I told her to go. Yet, I could no longer enjoy the pain I'd been so intent on inflicting.

A single bullet to the head finished the job for me, information be damned. I'd find another way to tie Abel and Titan together if needed for later.

Following Olivia wasn't my original intention, but as soon as I walk into my apartment and find her, I know this is where I want to be.

Seeing my raven sitting on the shower floor, still fully clothed, reignites every bit of rage I felt those three days hunting for Abel. Though, the moment she realizes I'm there and she rises, I know she's stronger than I've given her credit for.

Her thumb strokes my cheek, and a shudder rocks me to my core at her gentle touch. "You killed him."

"I did," I confirm without an ounce of regret.

"For me," she adds, an air of acceptance in her words.

She's not wrong. I wouldn't ever be able to rest again until I knew she no longer had to be afraid. Until I had set things as right as I could.

"He didn't deserve to breathe another day for touching what's...you." I almost say "what's mine", but I know I don't have that right.

Olivia isn't mine. Not in the way I've grown to crave but had been refusing to admit. I know I could claim her, but I'm not that kind of monster. I know this woman deserves better than the life I've dragged her into.

She lifts both hands and attempts to remove my bloodied shirt, but I stop her, placing my hand over hers. "What do you think you're doing?"

"Cleaning up the mess," she says, staring up at me

with an intensity I'm not sure I can deny. Not when I know how she's been hurting. "I figure it's the least I can do after thinking you're nothing more than an inconsiderate bastard who left me alone because he couldn't handle a broken woman."

I cradle her face in my palms, holding her softly, yet speaking firmly. "There is nothing broken about you, Raven."

Her eyes glaze over, and she shakes her head, leaning toward me and resting her forehead against my chest.

"I wanted to watch him die," she admits, seeming almost reluctant with her words. "Hell, I might have even been willing to kill him myself. I don't know what's happening to me, but what's worse is that I can't find anything wrong with those thoughts."

I hold her tightly against me, mindful that her body could still be bruised and battered from the encounter I'm certain has forever changed this woman. "There isn't anything wrong with those thoughts," I assure her. "He deserved to die. You're not the only person he's hurt."

She begins to shake within my arms, her vulnerability twisting my insides. I bring her closer to me, desperate to keep her intact when it seems as if she might fall apart right here in my arms.

"Will you wash me?" she asks so quietly that I'm not sure I've heard right. "I keep trying to rid myself of his stench from my body, but I can't do it on my own."

I should tell her no. I don't want to take advantage of her fragile state, but when she looks up at me with big doe eyes, so full of trust, I can't deny her. Not this or anything else she might ask for.

Without uttering another word, I gently trail my fingers down her arms and first remove the bandage around her wrist, letting it drop to the ground with an audible thud. Her shirt comes off next, revealing nothing beneath the loose fabric. Though, knowing how she's been hurt, I don't let my eyes linger where they want to.

I lower to my knees for her, carefully lifting each foot as she steadies herself by placing her good hand on my shoulder. Shoes and socks go next, and when I glance up to make sure she's certain that she wants me to continue, I see a conviction in her eyes that she needs this moment. She needs the gentle touch of a man to replace the beating she received.

It's not the soap that will remove the stench she speaks of, it's a new memory. One that won't remind her of what almost happened and that won't bring her closer to her nightmares, but further away from them.

With this understanding, I curl my fingers around the top of her leggings, guiding the wet fabric and her underwear down her hips, past her thighs, until they pool around her ankles.

My focus remains steadfast on the task at hand. Despite the temptation to admire her naked form, to revel in the ethereal beauty before me, I remind myself that this is not a moment for desire. It's one for solace, for tenderness, for helping her regain a sense of safety and self.

I might enjoy killing those who threaten all that I've created and strive to protect, but this woman doesn't need that man right now. She needs a side of me very few have ever seen, and, for the first time in years, I want someone to see it. I want to show her that I'm not the devil she may believe me to be.

Rising to my feet, I reach behind her, retrieving the soap and allowing it to fill my hands. Rubbing my palms together, I create a lather before placing them on her shoulders. The bubbles caress her neck as I fix my gaze on my raven, ensuring nothing has changed from her previous desires. Her eyes remain locked with mine, a silent affirmation accentuated by a subtle nod as she pulls the corner of her lower lip between her teeth.

My touch traverses her shoulders, only lightly trailing over the marks on her skin inflicted by the man I just eliminated. I suppress the fury that still simmers within me, recognizing that my anger has no place in this moment. What Olivia needs most right now is not my vengeance, but a gentle touch to mend her wounded soul.

My fingers lead the way down her arms, then back up again, sweeping lightly over her chest, then down her stomach. Leaving one hand on her hip, I reach for more soap before turning her until she gives me her back.

She moves further under the warm spray of the shower, washing away the bubbles I've left behind as I add more over her spine and ribs.

Olivia takes a step closer to me, pressing her back against my chest, and I keep my arms at my sides, waiting for her guidance. The weight of her body melds with mine as she seems to find solace in my warmth.

"Hold me, please," she whispers, her voice still carrying a heavy weight. "I need to feel safe again."

The last place I thought this woman would ever feel *safe* is in my arms, but denying her isn't something I'm capable of. Not after fearing for her life as I did.

My hands move around her stomach, pressing her tightly to my still-clothed body, hopeful that she can't feel how hard I am just from having her close like this.

Her fingers grasp my wrists, guiding one of my hands until it rests between her breasts, a gesture of trust and surrender. As I apply gentle pressure against her skin, she melts into me, her weight shifting, and I become her anchor, supporting her both physically and emotionally.

"Thank you, Luca," she says softly, her words laced with gratitude that I don't feel worthy of. Not after the way I've treated her, even while I've known I wanted her.

"I don't deserve your thanks," I reply gruffly. "I'm the reason you're hurting."

But Olivia shakes her head against my chest, the defiance I've continued to appreciate about her palpable. "You're also the reason I'm not buried beside my mother right now."

Though I'm aware that I saved her life in that alley, I don't welcome her praise. Not when I know I never should have let her leave the compound, knowing there are people out there that likely still wish her harm.

Claiming Olivia as mine might be the worst thing for her and filled with complications I'm not prepared for, but I can no longer deny the possessive instinct toward this woman that burns within me. No one has the right to harm what belongs to me without facing a vengeance that matches their transgressions.

And Titan Moretti will feel my wrath by the time I'm done seeking the retribution I so fiercely desire.

17

OLIVIA

When I forced myself out of the apartment in all my fury earlier, I never could have predicted the events that followed. Especially not Luca coming after me once I found him, and me, against all logic, pleading him to take care of me. Hell, I even assumed I'd feel regret after the way I asked him to take care of me, but there's a peace rooting at my core that won't allow anything of the sort.

With the warring emotions inside me, I can't find a reason to care any longer that this man is a murderer. That he masquerades as a businessman while secretly dabbling in the dark dealings of the mafia, beyond the realm of just inflicting harm on those who cross their path, seems irrelevant now.

I needed him to erase the memories of the last couple days more than anything else. Even if it had only been for the moment, sharing the shower with him, feeling how gentle he could be, and seeing the restraint he portrayed as he touched me with nothing other than compassion and understanding...

I'm no longer a woman trying not to fall for her captor.

Denying that I don't desperately want this man is nearly impossible. More accurately, I'm too tired to want to even try.

I stepped out of the shower after taking what solace I could from Luca and left him to finally undress and wash himself. The urge to stay and care for him, as I initially intended, is strong, but I'm not ready. Not yet.

I may have no problem admitting I care more for this man than I should, but I can't throw myself at him just because he's shown me a moment of kindness. I'm not an idiot. Emotionally traumatized and in need of companionship? Sure. But that doesn't have to include sex. At least, not right now.

Not until I know I'm ready. He may have been interrupted before reaching his intended goal, but the echoes of that threat still linger within me even after the man is dead.

Once I'm dressed and Luca remains in the bathroom, I settle in the living room on the couch. I tuck my feet beneath me, clutching a sketch pad in my hands that I haven't desired to hold in three long days.

This time, the pencil refuses to draw flowers. Instead, it yearns to capture the flecks of gold that occasionally shimmer in Luca's cognac eyes. It craves to immortalize the sharpness of his jaw adorned with the stubble that I find undeniably more attractive than his usual clean-shaven appearance.

Before I can decide whether to indulge the drawing impulse at all, Justine knocks twice on the front door and enters without waiting for me to respond. It's a habit she's acquired since I've been alone these past few days, though I doubt Luca would approve if he knew.

She stops abruptly, her gaze scanning me with curiosity. "Care to tell me what happened?" she questions, her arms crossed.

I tilt my head to the side, feigning ignorance. "What do you mean?"

She has no problem pointing out the obvious, though her tone is laced with concern. "You're wearing a bra. You haven't done that since..."

Her sentence trails off, the unspoken words hanging heavy in the air. We both know what she means.

"I'm feeling better," I offer as my only response. Justine may have swiftly become a friend, but I'm not in the mood to divulge the events that transpired between Luca and me.

Her eyebrows arch, and she crosses the room to sit beside me on the couch. "Because you know that Abel is dead?"

"How do you know that?" I counter, suddenly conscious that she could have seen me leaving or returning from the sublevels. Had she also seen Luca trailing after me?

She moves closer, sitting on the couch with me and keeping her eyes fixed on mine. "Jaxon was down there when you arrived. He told me that you witnessed that bastard being tortured by Luca. He also mentioned that it seemed like you had a hint of bloodlust yourself."

Of course, he'd seen that on my face.

"Wouldn't you if the man who wanted to violate you was at your disposal?" I ask pointedly. "Doesn't matter, though. Luca asked me to leave, and I did."

She stares harder at me, as if she knows I'm hiding a dirty secret. "Right."

There's a thud against the wall that I can only assume is the bathroom door opening in Luca's room. We both look toward his door until I feel Justine's grasp around my wrist.

"Careful," I tell her, but then realize that was just instinctual. The injury no longer hurts, and I'm more than grateful for that little reminder to be gone.

Her eyes move between me and the bedroom. "Luca came back."

I don't reply. It's not a question and not something I care to comment on just yet.

Justine stands and grins. "Alright. I'll play your little game. For now. Enjoy the privacy while it lasts. I'll be back later with your phone so you can help me placate your friends again. They've been blowing up your phone the last twelve hours. Especially that Tori chick. She's threatening to file a missing person's report if she doesn't speak directly with you by end of day."

I sigh. I should be grateful, and a part of me still is, that Tori cares so much about me, but I already have enough shit to deal with. I don't have the energy to pretend everything is okay while speaking with someone who knows me so well. Sandi is easier. While I consider her a friend, there's never been an emotional closeness between us.

Tori, on the other hand... She's been like a sister for more years than I can currently count.

"I'm sure I'll be right here when you return," I say to Justine as she heads toward the door.

She glances back at me, eyes pinched at the sides. "Normally, I'd believe you, but something tells me things are about to change. Either way, I'll find you. You can't get away from me that easily."

I chuckle at her response, finding solace in the fact that she thinks I would deliberately avoid her. Though I may crave some temporary solitude to guard my secrets, it doesn't mean I no longer value the friendship she has extended since that first day of my captivity.

After Justine departs, Luca emerges from the bedroom, clad in fresh charcoal slacks and a crisp white dress shirt. The sleeves are rolled up, just as he had them earlier, but there isn't a speck of blood in sight on the new shirt. As if he hadn't just committed murder in his basement.

A few days ago, such a thought would have sent revulsion coursing through me. Now, however, I find myself more intrigued than ever by the enigma that is Luca Monroe. Especially after glimpsing a more savage part of me.

There's a morally grey area inside me now that I didn't think existed. Yet, I can't deny the satisfaction that continues to grow within me knowing my attacker is dead. Even more, I wish I'd fought Luca and chosen to stay just a few minutes longer.

He eyes the front door, then shifts his gaze back to me. "What did Justine want?" he asks with an undercurrent of tension.

"She was checking in on me," I reply. "She's come by a lot since I've been alone."

The words slip out sharper than intended, a subtle jab at Luca's absence. I can't help that I feel a pang of resentment still. Just because I now understand why he was too busy to return doesn't mean that I'm not frustrated to have been left alone. He must have found time to sleep in the past few days, so why not in his own bed?

Luca pauses near the dining table, and I expect him to say something, to apologize for not being there after the attack, or offer some sort of further explanation.

My expectations aren't met, though. Silence stretches between us, and it feels as if he'd prefer to dismiss the ordeal I went through. That's how I interpret it, at least.

I rise from the couch, crossing my arms and piercing him with a glare. "You've got to be kidding me right now," I say as calmly as I can muster since I'm at least grateful for what he did do. Yet, I can't disregard my own emotions. Not when it feels as if everything has changed for me, and he seems content to remain...just as he's been.

"What?" he finally asks.

With a heavy sigh, I reply, "You're not even going to apologize?"

His sharp eyes slowly, yet with almost calculated effort, meet my hardened stare. "You want me to say sorry for spending three days hunting the piece of shit that hurt you? Would you have rather I been here, consoling you, while doing nothing to make sure he paid for what he did?"

I know he's right. I wouldn't have wanted him to stay by my side, but being ignored, left in the dark, wasn't okay either. I also can't deny that there's a part of me, a part that craves something more from Luca—something I don't even fully understand myself.

Given I'm not even sure what I want, I move back to the couch, landing on the cushions with a huff. "Just forget I said anything."

The echo of his heavy steps fill the room, but I don't turn his way, which seems to further piss him off, based on the grumbling mumbles I hear coming from him.

Luca stands in front of me, refusing to lower himself to my level as he speaks. "I'm not some prince charming who's going to dote on you, Little Raven," he says, his voice tinged with a mix of frustration and determination. "I showed you affection in the shower because you needed it. But something tells me that you're going to survive just fine without an apology for something I'm not sorry I did. If you were that lonely, you could have asked Justine to stay with you. Yet, you didn't. There isn't a single part of me that regrets what I did or not being in this room with you. If that's not good enough for you, then that's your problem, not mine."

Mother fuck fuck.

Is he being a dick? Absolutely. Am I possibly expecting more than I should, considering I'm understanding more and more about this man? Probably. But that doesn't mean my feelings aren't valid and that I shouldn't have the chance to express them. If I'm going to allow myself to care for Luca, then I can't let him control me or my emotions. I still need to be me.

"You could have told me what you were doing," I say with a conviction that forms from deep within me. "You didn't have to ignore me for days, making me feel as if I might be to blame for allowing myself to be attacked. Hell, you could have passed a message from Jaxon to Justine to me. Anything would have been better than being left to my own tortuous thoughts."

As I meet his steely gaze, I notice a flicker of acknowledgment in his eyes. His lips downturn, and the tension in his jawline betrays the strain of his clenched teeth.

"I'm not sorry for what I did," he repeats, his voice softer this time, almost as if he's relenting.

"And that's fine, Luca. You don't even have to apologize for leaving me in the dark, just don't fucking do it again." As the words escape my lips, I realize they also carry an admission—that there might be a next time, that I have no immediate plans to run away from this place.

The thought twists and turns in my stomach, leaving me unsure whether it's a good thing or bad. I swore this life wasn't for me, that I could never find comfort in a mafia family that thrives on violence and lawlessness, one that believes it can play God with the lives of others.

Yet...I know my attraction to the man standing before me is real. Even more, I'm certain he feels something for me in return, even if there may not be many moments that he shows it like he did in the shower.

"I'm going to go find you another wrap for your wrist," he says, confirming what I already assumed—this man doesn't apologize easily, if at all.

Uncertainty begins to cloud my mind. I have no idea if I can truly stay in this place, or if Luca even wants me to. But as I weigh my options, I come to a resolute decision—I don't care. Despite everything, I know I'm safe within the confines of this compound. I know Luca will do whatever it takes to ensure my safety, and as long as that remains true, I have no reason to rush into any hasty decisions.

Well, except for one that I've already made: Luca Monroe is worth getting to know. At least, as much as he'll allow me to. There will come a time when I'll have to evaluate if what he's capable of giving is enough to accept all the complexities and dangers that come with caring about the leader of a mafia family.

But that's a problem for future me to tackle, and right now, I'm not looking out for her. Present me demands the most attention, and I'm okay with that.

For now. Just like everything else lately, I can only deal with one moment at a time.

18

LUCA

Throughout my life, I've guarded myself against weaknesses. It's a fundamental principle ingrained into me by my father, a necessary survival tactic—as he called it—in this twisted world I choose to remain in.

Until now, I've never once regretted that choice. Maintaining an emotional distance has allowed me to excel at my job, surpassing all expectations. But now, everything has changed. Now, I have this woman in my apartment—one who stumbled into my life, blissfully unaware of the dangers that lurk within it. And the more I observe her, the more I question the possibility that she possesses a strength I didn't anticipate before.

The vulnerability I showed Olivia in the shower wasn't a mere impulsive act. Every word I spoke, every touch I bestowed upon her, held a genuine intention. Yet, I'm cautious not to raise her expectations to unrealistic heights.

When I informed her that I would never apologize, I expected her to react with anger or tears, like a petulant child. But she surprised me once again, accepting my unapologetic nature without protest. Her ability to acknowledge my flaws and still be drawn to me is somewhat remarkable. However...

Not denying my attraction to her and being who she deserves are two different things, but I'm selfish enough not to give a fuck. If my raven wants to stay here, then I'll gladly keep her. Even after the threat to her life is gone.

I'm fully aware that keeping her will leave her exposed to a continuous string of lingering threats. I've made the decision, though, and it's one I no longer wish to go back on—Olivia Danes is mine, and as long as she embraces that truth, she will remain by my side.

I don't need months to decipher my desires; I knew the moment I laid eyes on her when she stepped onto that stage and again when she walked into that alleyway—this woman is special. Beyond that, her audacity to fearlessly confront me, to express her true feelings despite knowing what I'm capable of, is undeniably sexy.

Her strength is something I overlooked before, but I won't make that mistake again.

After retrieving another wrap for her wrist from our medical closet, I go back to the room, intent on staying there for the rest of night. Not because she needs me, but because I'm tired as fuck and hungry.

Hunting Abel for three days meant that sleep and food were low on my list of priorities. Now that I'm not so singularly focused, I know I need to take a break.

Olivia is still on the couch when I return, her sketch pad back in her lap with her knees propped up, creating the angle she needs to draw without being hunched over. Strands of her damp onyx hair are tucked behind her ears, allowing her unwavering gaze to fixate on the task at hand, seemingly unaware of my return.

Curiosity piqued, I approach her, longing to discover the subject that has captivated her attention so intensely. But just as I'm about to glimpse the details of her work, she gasps, hurriedly flipping the pages away. "What are you doing?" she questions, her voice betraying her guilt.

I loom over her, narrowing my gaze. "What are *you* doing?"

"Nothing." Her reply is swift, but the lie is evident.

Extending my hand, I demand, "Give me the paper, Raven."

"No." Her grip tightens, her knuckles turning white.

"That's not a word you should use with me," I warn, seizing the drawing from her grasp with force. "Ever."

I find what I'm looking for, and one glance at her artwork renders me speechless. She's sketched my face, or rather, my eyes. They peer back at me with an intensity that leaves me uncertain of my own emotions. Though devoid of color, her detailed lines and markings bring forth a striking resemblance, every nuance flawlessly captured.

She's no longer looking at me, and her hair shields half of her face as she stares toward the windows across the room.

Instead of continuing to make her uncomfortable, I

hand the paper back and say nothing. Not because I don't appreciate that she's made me look anything other than the murderer she's seen me to be, but because I choose not to push further.

I pull the wrap for her wrist from my back pocket and hand it to her. "You should put that on."

Her wide, innocent eyes look back up me, making my chest ache from the ferocious desire I have to protect this woman. To make sure that nobody can ever harm her in any way for as long as she'll allow.

The emotions are so strong that I have to force myself to breathe through them before I do or say something that would make me a liar.

No matter how much I want to protect this raven from those who wish her harm, I know that it's more likely I'll be the one to destroy her in the end. Even if it's not by my hand, I'll still somehow be to blame.

As I start to pour myself a drink at the bar, she says, "Thank you."

"For what?" I turn toward her with a tumbler between my fingers and rest my hip lightly against the counter.

She raises the bandage. "For this." Her cheeks flush as she pauses. "Though, I don't really think I need it any longer, but also thanks for coming back to the room after I sort of yelled at you."

"You're welcome," I say, taking a long pull from my whiskey.

Her responding chuckle isn't what I expect to hear

next. "I see you can choose to have manners when it suits you."

"If you haven't learned yet, I only do what I want." I finish my drink and add, "In all aspects of my life."

Olivia swallows roughly, her gaze drifting toward her drawing pad, which now displays a page filled with previously sketched flowers. "Is there somewhere here that I can paint? Justine brought me some acrylics, but I don't want to make a mess in your space."

Apart from seeking an apology earlier, I believe this is the first time she's requested anything since arriving in my apartment. A fact that has escaped my attention until now.

"We'll sort something out soon," I assure her. "You're also welcome to move through the compound as you want. Nobody will stop you from going anywhere that isn't off limits."

"Like the sublevels?" she asks, again allowing her teeth to tug at her lips. Lips that I've imagined on more than one occasion around my cock.

I want to tell her yes, but I saw the flicker of desire in her eyes when she realized what I was doing to Abel. It may have been brief, but the thrill of the torture he was about to endure triggered something inside her.

"While you did make me realize we need better security where the stairs are concerned, I'll leave that choice up to you," I say before grabbing my phone from my pocket. "I'm ordering dinner. Are you hungry?"

Her tongue darts out, unconsciously wetting her lips as

she stares at me with a hunger I yearn to satiate. Leaning further back against the couch, she brushes her hair away, her eyes locked on mine as she says, "Famished."

Fucking hell.

I was trying to do the right thing by her in the shower earlier, but if she continues to beckon me with her eyes, practically pleading with me to fuck her, I won't be able to hold back. At least, not with everything.

When she's ready for everything, she'll have to use her words. Not just actions.

19

OLIVIA

Sweat drips down my temples, my chest heaves, and my legs burn with an intensity I'm certain I've never felt. Yet, I can't stop running. The pain brings me a relief I didn't expect when Justine dragged my ass down to the gym a few days ago.

She said I was a little too tense and should exert some energy. If only she knew how right she was.

After the shower and proceeding conversation with Luca about whatever is going on between us, he's buckled down with work...or whatever it's called when mafia kings do mafia-like stuff, and I've rarely seen him in the last four days.

Worse, he hasn't touched me. Not even a passing brush in the moments we're in the same room. I'm not sure what to think, but I do know that running on this treadmill has shown me that exercise isn't as evil as I previously assumed.

Though, the rising tension that continues to throb at

my core has hardly eased. The only things I've been able to get under control with a few trips to the gym are my thoughts.

When I'm running, I don't overthink the craziness of everything that's happened in the last few weeks. I consider the facts and accept that there is nothing I can do to change what's happened, but what I can do is prepare myself for what's to come.

I don't get lost in the treadmill the whole time, though. I also spend a decent portion of my newfound gym time with the weights and punching bag, learning how to use my body as a weapon so that nobody can ever use it against me again.

That brings me more solace and motivation than anything else ever could.

Knowing Abel is dead has relieved me of the nightmares, but I know he's not the only person to wish me harm. Letting my guard down isn't an option. Pretending everything is going to go back to normal one day after all I've seen is a fairytale that I won't allow myself to live in.

Justine's hand slams down on the red button in front of me. "Time for your beating." Her sinister smile frightened me the first time, but it hasn't taken me long to match her thrill.

We don't actually beat on each other, but that doesn't mean we don't feel the impact when one of us pounds on the bag and the other is holding it or when we use the punching gloves and hand mitts to practice our right hooks.

She's already wearing the gloves, meaning it's my turn to put the mitts on. As soon as I lift my protected palms into the air, she strikes, and it takes every bit of strength to keep my legs from stumbling back.

Justine doesn't let up, either. She throws hit after hit, punching until her arms are shaking and sweat trickles down her chest. "I think I'm done for the day, but I can hold the punching bag for you if you want."

I shake my head, reaching for my water bottle. "I got enough punching in before the treadmill. I'm going to go shower and then have dinner."

She uses a towel to wipe her face, then frowns. "I'd join you, but I have plans with Jaxon tonight."

Oh, how I envy her.

"It's all good," I assure her. "I'll see you tomorrow morning. Have enough fun for the both of us." My tone is teasing, but on the inside, I'm already wondering if we're at the point in our friendship that I could ask her to get me a toy that would at least ease the ache deep inside me.

She laughs and nudges my shoulder. "I bet Jax wouldn't mind if you came home with me."

"I'm not that desperate," I chuckle, adding, "Yet."

Our laughter fills the gym as we exit and head toward the elevator. "Luca will come...around soon," she jokes. "Maybe just stop getting dressed for the day."

It's an idea that immediately has merit, but I dismiss it just as quickly. I won't show him that he has power over me to make me desperate for his touch. No, at this point, I'll go upstairs and take care of my own needs with my hand, something I should have done days ago. I'd held off after the trauma of what happened at the nightclub and needing time to process.

I thought it would take longer, but with my nightmares gone, my sexual appetite doesn't seem to understand the word no.

Another thing I can blame on Luca.

Justine leaves me to get out on the third floor, and I continue up to the fourth. I barely have the door shut behind me before I'm stripping off my clothes, heading straight for the shower.

I twist the faucet handle, releasing a stream of water. I quickly untie my hair, take a fresh towel from the nearby shelf and hang it on the hook, then check the temperature of the spray with my toe before committing to step in. I can feel the warmth spread through my tense and sore muscles as I ease myself into the shower.

Rinsing off the sweat comes first, then I fill my palm with Luca's body wash. As I rub the lather of bubbles under my arms, then over my shoulders and down my chest, I can't help from squeezing a little harder around my breasts that ache nearly as much as my deprived pussy.

Moving further under the spray, I wash away the soap and let my hands wander downward, past my hips before spreading my lower lips apart with my middle finger as it searches for the bundle of nerves that needs some serious loving.

Using circular motions, I rub over my clit, my body already shivering with the anticipation of release. Stepping back, I rest my head and back against the tile wall and close my eyes, inhaling Luca's sandalwood scent from the lingering soap and remembering when he was in here with me. How he meticulously undressed me, cleansed my body of all that I wished to forget, and made me feel more cherished than I have in my entire life.

I imagine him still kneeling before me, lifting my leg and dragging his tongue along my center over and over again until I cry out, all while demanding more from me as he devours my body, commanding every inch until I've melted beneath his hands.

Only when I can barely breathe from need, when my legs shake so badly that I can hardly stand, do I open my eyes, water droplets clinging to my lashes. But I find myself still alone in the steaming shower, and it's not Luca's tongue lavishing my pussy, it's my own hand.

A disappointing reality to return to, but that doesn't stop me from finishing the job or letting my eyelids flutter closed once more so that I can return to the fantasy I've conjured.

This time, it's no longer Luca's face between my legs, but his hard cock, and when he thrusts inside me, I see stars.

"Harder, Luca," I beg, so close to the orgasm I know I won't survive without.

"How hard can you handle, Raven?"

The heady words wash over me, and I moan again, proud of how real this moment feels. How close he sounds and how his warmth wraps around me, drawing me further into the moment I only wish was true.

With a curl of my own fingers and extra pressure on

my clit, I'm seconds away from a fiery release when I feel a steady touch on my shoulder that begins to travel down the arm of the hand currently between my legs.

A scream is seconds from ripping out of my lungs as I open my eyes. Only, no sound escapes from between my lips. Instead, they form into an "O" of surprise, and I blink rapidly, tempted to slap myself across the face to be certain this is real.

Luca stands just inches away from me, naked as the day he was born and fucking glorious. Well, all except for the dark spots of something I'm nearly certain is blood dotting his face and hands.

Still, I don't let that deter me. My gaze sweeps over his broad shoulders, then down his muscled chest and stomach to find his cock standing at attention.

My tongue darts out, imagining what it would be like to taste him, but before I can make a move, Luca is invading my space, picking me up and pressing my back harder against the tile wall. "I asked you a question, and you didn't answer me."

His tone is forceful, but there isn't a part of me that is afraid. He might be a murderer, but if there's one thing that I'm certain of right now, Luca will never lay a hand on me. Not to hurt me.

I try to think back to his question, but considering I thought I was daydreaming, I'm not sure what I'm supposed to be answering.

"How long were you watching me?" I ask, trying to change the conversation as I tighten my legs around his waist.

"Long enough." His fingers dig into my ass cheeks. "I asked you how hard can you handle, Raven, and I expect an answer. You don't get to make yourself come in my shower without my permission. If you want it harder, and you're saying my name, then it may as well be me that gives you the release you desire. But you need to tell me. What do you want from me? My fingers, my mouth, my cock?"

Before I can answer, his face is moving closer to mine, and I prepare for him to kiss me, but instead, his head tilts to the side and he drags his tongue up the column of my neck. His teeth scrape over my sensitive skin, and another moan escapes from my lips.

"Are you going to answer me, Raven? Or are you going to merely tremble in my arms until I've grown bored?" he grumbles in my ears.

I grind myself over his stomach, impatient for the release I was so fucking close to claiming before he interrupted me. More than that, I just need for him to actually touch me where I need it most.

"I want your cock," I finally say with a confidence that surprises even me. "I want you to fuck me, Luca. Right here, right now, in this shower until I can't see straight."

He grips my chin between his fingers and doesn't speak until he seems certain he has my full attention. "You're absolutely sure that's what you want? What you can handle?"

My hips tilt forward, desperate for any kind of

friction they give my throbbing center. "More sure than I am about anything else in my life right now."

The rumble that echoes from his chest has my breaths coming faster.

Luca doesn't hesitate a second time in following through on my command. He lifts me higher until his cock is positioned at my pussy. I wiggle in his grasp, needing to feel him stretching my insides more than I've ever needed anything else.

"Are you on birth control?" he asks, and I've never been thankful in my life for the sliver of plastic in my arm.

I point to the spot to show him proof. "Two more years of it right here."

"Good answer." He surges his hips upward, and I cling to his shoulders, throwing my head back and crying out as he fills me so thoroughly that I'm certain my imagination would have never been able to touch the reality of this moment.

"Fuck," I hiss, rocking against him as if my life depends on fucking him until I can't see straight.

Luca holds tightly to my hips, keeping our bodies aligned as he watches me fall apart in his arms.

"You like that?" he asks, thrusting faster and faster while I hang on for dear life.

All I can do is nod as I squirm against him, pushing my clit hard against his pelvic bone until sparks fly behind my eyelids. My panting cries fill the shower as I ride him hard, drawing out the orgasm I can sense right at its precipice.

Luca's jaw tightens, and his hold on me intensifies, showing me his own release isn't far behind. His fingers move to grasp one of my nipples, pinching hard until I moan louder, clenching around his thick cock.

I want to hold off, to draw this moment out, but that's not possible. Not this time. And now that I've had him this once, it better not be the fucking last. Mafia king be damned.

"So close," I mutter, increasing my movement as I accept the pounding he's giving me without a single regret. My cries grow louder, and I squeeze my eyes shut when the spots in my vision become too distracting.

My release leaps off the metaphorical cliff, and I'm pretty sure I'm screaming my pleasures away at this point, but there's not a part of me that gives a damn about how loud I am.

Luca's thrusts come harder and faster until he drops his head against my chest, shuddering against me and finding his own release.

Most of my body tingles with ecstasy as I cling to Luca, resting my head against his shoulder while the aftershocks of one hell of an orgasm move through me.

Yet, all too soon, he lowers me back to the ground, and my feet are forced to find their balance on the tile floor of the shower. Still, I lean against the wall, not ready to exert more effort than I need to.

Luca steps under the spray of the surprisingly still-hot water and quickly washes up. I'm not even halfway to a full recovery by the time he's done.

When he steps out of the shower without a word or

even a kiss, I can't be mad about it. Not even when I realize he didn't once press his lips to mine. He gave me exactly what I asked for when I told him to fuck me.

Even though I was momentarily distracted, I haven't forgotten that he had blood on him when he first stepped into the shower.

Something that, at least right now, seems a little more important than a kiss.

20

LUCA

When I entered the bathroom after coming home, I never expected to find Olivia there, her soft moans echoing my name. I have no idea how long she'd been in there before my arrival, but the sight of her through the glass, obscured by steam, sent a surge of heat through me. It was easily one of the most arousing things I've yet to witness.

I hadn't thought she was ready for more, and with how busy I've been, I had no intentions of touching her until I could be certain. But as soon as the words "Fuck me, Luca" left her lips, there was no denying myself what we both desired—my cock driving into her waiting pussy.

Fucking her was better than the finest aged whiskey, intoxicating and addictive. The way she clung to my body and rode me without holding anything back. By how openly she speaks to me, I shouldn't have thought she'd be any other way, but still, she manages to take me by surprise nearly every day that she's here.

I leave her in the shower to finish washing up on her own while I dispose of my bloodied clothes. It hadn't been my intention to kill anyone today, but I've spent many of my days lately hunting for men who have crossed me, and my patience isn't what it normally is.

Using Abel's phone, we found the messages between him and Titan, gaining the connection I wanted to justify my killing the other mafia leader. By proving that Titan broke an unspoken code of not crossing those who aren't disrupting your business, I can easily take over his territory. Anyone else will think twice about challenging me.

Though, I won't keep his businesses for long once I have them. Drugs haven't ever been, and won't ever be, something I want to be involved in. And I'm rather certain he has a string of women that he whores out, likely against their will. At least I'll be able to shut that down.

As long as I can locate the fucker.

Despite our extensive connections, including those within law enforcement, none of the tips we've received have proven useful. Today seemed to be our closest chance at finding Titan, but the only person present in the warehouse was a nobody who foolishly pretended to be more significant than he was.

Lies don't typically get anyone far in life, especially not with me.

As I walk back into the bedroom, having disposed of my stained suit, Olivia emerges from the bathroom. A white cotton towel is tightly wrapped around her chest, and her long, wet hair clings to her shoulders as she gazes at me.

I expect to find affection in her gaze after the release I gave her, but all I see is suspicion.

"Why did you have blood on you?" she asks, making no move to get dressed.

"Can we have this conversation once you're dressed?" Her nakedness only serves to bring about my desire to bend her over the bed and fuck her again.

"Do you lack so much self-control that you can't speak to a woman unless she's clothed?" Her words push me, and while I should be annoyed, I find myself strangely entertained.

Advancing toward her, each step deliberate, I loom over her petite frame, my gaze burning into hers. "I maintain control in all things, Raven."

"Then why did you have blood on you?" she presses, her tone devoid of even a hint of fear.

Fuck, the way that affects me shouldn't be allowed.

"Because I ran out of patience, not control," I reply, stepping away from her before I do something I don't have time for.

She makes a humming noise from the back of her throat. "Right. So, why did you run out of *patience*? You've been gone a lot and haven't said why."

I cast a quick glance back at her before walking into my closet. "You haven't asked."

"Well, I'm asking now."

Taking my time, I grab a tie and drape it around my neck before pulling a suitcoat from its hanger and carrying it back into the bedroom with me. Just as I'm about to set the coat on the bed, Olivia drops her towel as she stands in front of the dresser with all her belongings in it.

It takes me a moment longer to continue what I'm doing and to answer her question. "Titan Moretti, the man who sent men to kill Senator McAdams, he also sent Abel after you."

She pauses mid-pull with her black lacy underwear stopping at her knees. With one deep breath, she resumes. "And now you've killed Titan?"

With frustration, I have to tell her no. "We haven't been able to find him. Today we thought we were getting closer, but the guy didn't know as much as he pretended to."

"But once you find Titan, you're going to kill him," she states, and I'm once again intrigued about her fascination with murder.

"Would that bring you happiness, Raven?" I ask, straightening my tie and giving her my full attention.

She stands on the opposite side of the bed from me, clad only in her underwear, but doesn't seem at all uncomfortable being nearly naked in my presence.

"What would make me happy is knowing that there aren't any more deranged men out there who want me dead," she declares. "To be free from feeling trapped would be wonderful."

A flicker of panic courses through me, but it vanishes as swiftly as it came. "You're not being forced to stay here. You can leave at any time."

Her laughter fills the room, harsh and bitter. "Right. Is that what you would prefer?" She turns her back to me, reaching for a pair of jeans on top of the dresser, but I don't allow her the opportunity to put them on.

I spin her until she's facing me again and pin her against the wooden surface just as I did on her first day in this room. "If I wanted you anywhere other than right where you are, then you would be there. As I told you before, I'm not your prince charming. I will disappoint you and I will hurt you, but as long as you're here, I will also protect you. It's up to you to decide if that's enough. Once you do, don't question your place here."

She nods, her eyes unmoving from my challenging stare. "Understood."

"Good, because I need to go," I reply. "I only came home to shower and change."

"Am I allowed to ask where you're going?"

I turn away from her to grab my suit coat from where I left it on the bed. "You can always ask."

This elicits a heavy sigh from her. "Where are you going now?"

"To Monroe," I answer freely. "They don't appreciate it when I fail to make appearances at least once every few days."

"And your employees, do they have any idea who you truly are?" she asks while resuming her dressing.

I shake my head. "They may have theories, but I've made sure there's never any concrete evidence of what I choose to do outside of Monroe."

"Why?"

Her question catches me off guard. It's just a single word, but no one has ever asked me why I've chosen to build my empire with two distinct lifestyles.

I'm not even sure I know, or that I want to know. It's just what I've done.

"Because I can," is all I say as I reach into my pocket. "I need to go, but I have something for you."

I hand her the phone she dropped in the alleyway and hasn't been able to have back since.

She blinks several times, clearly taken aback. "I can use this on my own?"

"Yes," I say pointedly. "I'm trusting you to know what you shouldn't say to anyone who asks where you've been. Make up whatever you want to appease your friends. You can even tell them the mysterious billionaire who bid on you has kept you away. Just maybe leave out the underground cell."

I know enough about women that if Olivia tells her friends she's been holed up with a man, they'll ask a lot less questions. Which I'd prefer. At least now she won't have to lie about having the best orgasm of her life. I don't need her to confirm that with words to know it's the truth.

Her lips thin as she rolls her eyes. "But the underground cell is the best part."

The sarcasm is clear in her tone, yet I still feel the need to taunt her. Reaching around her back, I jerk her forward until she's flush against my hard body. "I would have thought our time in the shower held that title."

Olivia's cheeks turn crimson, and she licks her lips,

leaning closer, but I don't have time to indulge her lingering needs. I release her and step back. "I'll be back later."

Without waiting for her response, I walk out of the bedroom only to hear her call after me.

"Bastard," she seethes.

I smirk, even though she can no longer see me. "You may not admit it, but you wouldn't want me any other way, Raven."

I'm out the door and locking it behind me before she can retort. The day had been challenging before I returned home, and it's unlikely to end on a positive note by spending the rest of the afternoon in the office. Yet, the grin on my face persists until I step out of the elevator into the parking garage.

Damon is waiting for me by the SUV, my driver for the remainder of the day since Jaxon requested the evening off.

"Ready?" he asks, leaning casually as if he hasn't been left waiting longer than I previously stated.

I nod curtly at Damon and slide into the backseat of the vehicle. The leather upholstery molds comfortably to my form as I settle in, preparing myself to go from murdering mafia leader to a well-respected CEO of a multi-billion-dollar company.

Normally, splitting my time isn't difficult, but the weariness of very little sleep and not enough downtime is catching up to me.

Titan needs to be found soon, or it just might be more than my patience that wears thin.

21

OLIVIA

After getting dressed, I collapse onto the bed, my body still buzzing from the intense and very unexpected shower session with Luca. I had no problems fantasizing about him touching me like that. Now that he has, yet still feels so...Luca, I'm not sure what to think.

Still, I know I can't dwell on those thoughts for long. Tori hasn't actually heard from me in weeks, even though she doesn't know that. I can't be selfish and make her wait any longer just because I allowed myself to fall for my captor.

I stare at her contact in my phone and desperately want to press on her name, but I also know I can't tell her everything and, what I will say, she's not going to understand. My best friend is going to think I've had a psychotic break after losing my mother and demand that I return.

If only things were that simple.

With a heavy sigh, I click on her phone number as I

lay flat on the bed. She'll forgive me one day when I can tell her the whole truth. Hopefully.

Tori's voice slices through the air, sharp with frustration, and I flinch at the impact of her words. "What the fuck, Liv?"

I really do hate that I've hurt her so deeply.

"I'm sorry," I offer sincerely. "More than you can possibly understand."

Before I can finish speaking, a video call request pops up on the screen. With reluctance, I accept, keeping the phone close to my face so she can't see too many details of Luca's bedroom.

"Where the hell are you? That bedding looks rather fancy for a cabin," she demands, a crease between her brows and dark circles under her hazel eyes.

Maybe I should have checked the messages shared between Tori and Justine first. Not that I don't trust Justine, but Tori is a sensitive soul, and my disappearance couldn't have been easy on her.

I realize too late that I'm not prepared for this conversation.

"I'm not at the cabin any longer," I reply, bracing myself for her reaction. "I'm sorry. I thought I told you when I left there."

Her lip lifts into a snarl. "You know, considering I'm supposed to be your best friend, you haven't been telling me much lately. Are you going to tell me where you are now?"

My chest aches as the lies push forward. I try to remind myself that I'm doing this for her protection. Tori can't know the mafia is real. At least not while there is still a very real threat over my head.

"I met someone," I reply, forcing myself to keep her hard stare. "He's been letting me stay with him so that I can figure my shit out."

The betrayal that sweeps across her face cuts me to the core. "Was my offer not good enough for you?"

"It's not like that, T," I protest, desperately attempting to mend the fracture between us. "I swear. I just... I managed to gather the funds through the auction Sandi set up for me, and I needed to escape."

"And quit your job and stop answering your phone and start seeing some stranger," she adds, each accusation slicing at my heart because of the half-truths they hold.

"Hurting you was never my intention," I implore, my voice laced with genuine regret. "Please believe me. I promise to answer my phone now and talk to you as often as possible."

"When are you coming home?" Her tone softens, the anger dissipating only momentarily.

"I don't know," I admit, feeling a pang of uncertainty.

She cuts me off before I can elaborate. "What the fuck do you mean you *don't know?* You have your mom's house here, filled with boxes and waiting for you. You have a job to get back and a life, Olivia. Losing your mom is devastating, and my heart breaks for you, but you can't let everything else slip away."

Confusion fills me about the mention of boxes. I hadn't once given all the shit in my old apartment a second thought. I have no idea how any of it got to my mom's, assuming my stuff is what's in the boxes, but I'm smart enough to know that now isn't the time to ask Tori if she knows how the items were moved into the house.

"I know none of this makes sense," I say, shifting to a more upright position. "But I promise I'm okay. Isn't that enough for now?"

My kind, sweet best friend has been through hell in the last few weeks, thanks to my absence. Not that I haven't been, but I won't dismiss the hurt I've caused her. I just need her to forgive me and trust that I'm doing what I need to.

Her lips flatten, and I'm certain she's going to keep yelling at me, but then her shoulders finally drop and she lets out a heavy sigh. "I guess, but when do I get to see you again? This is the longest we've been apart in decades."

"Soon," I promise and hope I'm not lying. "I just need to sort a few other things out before I can leave where I'm at."

"Like what?" she presses. "I've been checking in on things at your mom's, including the mail in case there were more bills, but it seems all of them have been paid in full. Plus, someone delivered all of your stuff to the house. Am I to assume the guy you're staying with did that for you? Do I even want to know why?"

I blink several times, unsure if I've heard her right. My bills were *all* paid in full? I just assumed Justine took care of the property taxes so that I didn't lose the house. How am I ever going to pay these people back if that's not the case? I don't know, which brings the fear of never having my freedom back to the forefront of my mind.

"I don't know," I answer her honestly. "I wasn't told my bills would be paid for like that. I just...I don't know."

She seems to have pity on me for a brief second as her eyes soften. "Are you in danger, Liv? Who is this guy? Did you know him before, or did you just happen to stumble upon him?"

I do my best to shake the stupor that's fallen over me. I need to sell this story. I need Tori not to worry and, more importantly, not to look for me. I don't know what I would do if she got herself wrapped up in all this with me.

"I met him the night of the auction," I reply and do my best to smile. "He won the winning bid for a date with me and wanted to go out that night. He drove me back to his place, we chatted, and he gave me a place to sleep. When I realized how nice it was to be somewhere I'd never been before, that didn't hold memories to make my grief feel like it might never end...I made casual mention to him the next morning that I wanted to get away and he offered up his cabin."

"And you just trusted him not to be a murderer?" she asks with raised brows.

"Oh, he definitely is," I tease, attempting to inject some lightheartedness. "Bloody hands every other day, that one."

She finally laughs, and I hate myself more than ever for pretending those words are pure fiction.

"Damn it, Liv." She shakes her head, fighting a grin.

"Please, don't disappear on me again. Texting wasn't enough these last few weeks."

Her voice cracks a little at the end, and I sense that there's something she's not telling me.

"Has anything else been happening while I've been away?" I ask softly, watching her face for any sort of tell that she may not reply with the truth.

"Nothing that's important right now," she says. "When can I see you? I assume Mr. Billionaire lives in Portland or did he fly you off to some extravagant place?"

The forcefulness of her excitement for me isn't missed and my heart aches. I want to push her for answers, but considering I'm keeping plenty of secrets of my own, I let things be what they are.

"Hopefully this next week," I reply. "I'll work out some plans just as soon as I can. I promise."

I hear the open and close of a door, and she glances to her left. "I need to go, but we'll talk again *soon*, right?"

"Very soon." It's a promise I shouldn't have to break now that I have my phone back.

"Love you, Liv," Tori says, the sadness back in her tone.

"Love you, too."

The video chat ends, and I slam my phone down on the mattress. Damn it. I need to figure out a way to meet with her sooner rather than later. I don't like that she's hiding something, too.

If it's her arrogant boyfriend causing her grief, he's about to have the shit literally scared out of him. I may have reservations about Justine using Jaxon's money to handle my bills, but using the guys to put some fear into Greg isn't above what I'm willing to do for my best friend.

Not even fucking close.

————

Having my phone back has a bittersweet sting. I spend hours scrolling through messages and photos, a masochistic dance of reminiscence and heartbreak. Tears fill my vision repeatedly, blurring the memories and intensifying the ache of loss. But it's not just the absence of communication with my friends that hurts.

It's the reminder that my mother is gone, irreversibly taken from my life. I crave to gaze at her smiling face in the photos, hoping to feel her presence, but it only amplifies the emptiness. There won't be any more phone calls. No shared lunches or dinners. No sleepovers. No... anything.

Overwhelmed, I collapse on the couch, clutching my phone to my chest as sobs wrack my body. Why her? Why did she have to be taken from me? Thoughts twist and spiral in my mind, a never-ending cycle of anguish and unanswered questions.

If she hadn't died, I wouldn't have known about her past-due bills. I wouldn't have gone to that auction or seen the dead body that now has another man wishing for me to be dead.

"Fuck," I mutter into the empty room, swiping furiously at my face. I don't want to be a mess. Hell, I'm not even sure I can afford to be. I need to draw on whatever strength I had when I was taken. The parts of me that allowed me to be brave in that cell, to stare a murderer in the face, and not break.

My phone gets shoved into the cracks of the cushion. As much as I want to be able to answer when Tori reaches out again, I need a break from all that lies within that thing.

I get up and decide to pour myself a shot of whiskey. Luca seems fond of the alcohol. Maybe I'm missing something by avoiding the stronger drink.

Flipping the crystal tumbler over, I grab the bottle and tip it slowly so that I don't get too much, wanting to avoid wasting anything I won't be able to force down if I hate the stuff.

Vodka I can handle, tequila only after I've had vodka, but anything else, unless it's been mixed with a lot of other sugary shit, I've avoided for reasons unknown.

Now, with my life in shambles, why shouldn't I?

As I lift the glass to my lips, the door swings open, and Luca strides in. His eyes dart around the room, panic flickering momentarily before his gaze lands on me, his eyebrows raised.

"Helping yourself, huh?" he remarks, stepping closer and shedding his suit coat.

"Not covered in blood tonight, huh?" I retort, grasping tightly to the resolve I'd just been searching for and lowering my glass for the moment.

When he gets closer, his gaze narrows. "What happened?"

"Nothing," I say. "I've been in this room since you left."

"I know that." His tone makes me wonder if he watches me while he's away...

"Why have you been crying?" he asks more assertively than the question should require.

The weight of the whiskey suddenly feels too heavy in my fingers. Luca isn't the type of man I envision to handle emotions well.

"It's just been a day."

He steps closer and grasps my elbow. "Did someone say something to you?"

"No. It was just a lot harder getting my phone back than I realized it would be," I finally admit, hoping not to draw this conversation out. "I don't think I said anything, but my mother died the week before I went to that auction."

Just as I assume, Luca isn't quick to console me. He releases my arm and pours his own drink before speaking again. "I'm sorry for your loss."

"Thank you," I reply, then clink my glass to his. "To overcoming all the shitty things."

He doesn't smile or even agree with my statement, but he at least drinks with me. While he does so silently, I make a God-awful noise, gagging but not giving up.

The smoky tinge to the liquid feels almost... aggressive. There's a hint of vanilla in there somewhere, but that does nothing to quell the burning that moves swiftly through my mouth and down my throat.

My eyes squeeze closed as I swallow the remainder of

the shot. Once I'm certain I won't throw everything back up, I reach for a bottle of water and quickly chug half of the contents.

"I take it you're not a connoisseur of alcohol," Luca says, a hint of amusement playing at his lips.

"I'd say not." The back of my hand wipes over my lips. "I'll stick to my fruity drinks from now on."

"Probably safest," he says with a slight hum.

He takes his suitcoat and heads to the bedroom. I follow like the lost little puppy I currently feel like.

"Do you know if Justine and Jaxon are still on their date?" I ask him as I lean against the bed and he goes to his closet.

"I gave him the night off," Luca answers. "They probably won't surface until morning."

Lucky her, I think.

"Why?" he asks when he gets done putting his clothes away.

I shrug, not wanting to get her in trouble for paying my bills with the mafia's money. "I just need to ask her about some things she was supposed to do on my behalf while I couldn't."

Luca steps closer, invading my personal space instead of returning to the living room as I anticipated. "What things?"

I swallow hard, meeting his intense gaze. "Paying some bills for me with my own money. I spoke to my friend Tori, and there seems to have been some confusion. I just want to sort it out."

He takes a step back, face devoid of emotion. "Was having all of your debts wiped clean not enough for you?"

My eyes bulge. Shit. He knows.

"That's not what I meant," I stammer. "It's too much. I can't pay her back for all of that. I just need to know how to make things right." Or preferably to reverse them.

"It's not her you need to pay back," he says, sending a chill down my spine.

"What do you mean?"

"I mean I paid your bills, Raven." He stands there unmoving while I'm doing everything I can not to have a panic attack. "Don't look so frightened by that. Your cooperation will be payment enough."

My cooperation? As if I haven't been a model kidnappee since being here. Well, mostly.

"Why?" is all I can think to ask as the situation sinks in.

"Because it's in my best interest to keep you from trying to escape and handle these things yourself," he says, as if that makes everything understandable.

"But why?" I press further. "You could have killed me and then still continued with your plans to kill Titan. Why did you keep me alive outside of thinking you could use me to keep him in check?"

"Why does it matter?" he counters, remaining still as ice, giving nothing away.

"Because it does. To me." I do my best to keep my voice strong, but it doesn't seem to make a difference.

He steps closer once again, towering over me, but I refuse to back down or cower. "That doesn't mean you get to know why. Haven't you learned by now that I do what I want?"

Before I can respond, to vent my fury at his arrogant comment, he swiftly turns and exits the room. I contemplate following him, ready to voice my opinion, but I stop myself, thinking better of it.

If he wants to goad me like that, I won't take the bait. Luca Monroe can fuck off if he thinks he can continue to treat me this way.

Fuck off all by his lonesome.

22

LUCA

Sleep eludes me. I didn't intend to be cruel to Olivia again, but I also didn't think that I was going to receive a text from Damon telling me that there's an actual price on Olivia's head.

He's already working on solutions to make sure the compound is as safe as possible, and I intended to tell Olivia that she needed to be more careful when I came back to the apartment, but seeing her already upset...

She was only supposed to be someone I bid on and never saw again. A temptation I wouldn't have the opportunity to act on. Her beauty and innocence, a fleeting attraction that I would eventually forget.

Yet, with her here, learning how strong she truly is while still just as innocent as I assumed, she's also not afraid of what lies within the shadows. It's a combination that seems to be my undoing.

I'll never tell her, but the more she fights back, the more I want to drop to my knees and worship her. It's not that I don't believe she should have that sort of control over me. It's more that the consequences of allowing myself to truly care that much could be more than I'm willing to pay.

Letting her all the way in and losing her would ruin me in ways I know I'm not prepared for.

Titan put a hundred-thousand-dollar price on her head. That sum won't attract anyone I can't handle, but it's enough to draw the attention of foolish individuals who believe breaching our sanctuary will be effortless.

The need to hold her close to me and make sure nobody can ever harm her intensifies, but for now, I settle for lightly brushing onyx strands of hair away from her face as I watch her sleep soundly next to me, no longer separated by the mountain of pillows that seemed to dwindle every day until just last week when she began sleeping at the head of the bed.

My staring goes on for much too long, and I'm nearly ready to roll over and close my eyes when she lets out a small moan. I tense, searching her face for any signs of pain in case she's having a nightmare. But instead of crying out in fear, her hand reaches across the bed, caressing my chest as she mutters my name so softly that I know it can't be anything bad.

My dick instantly hardens, and there's no sleeping for me now. I place my hand over hers and move it slowly up her arm. She practically purrs under my touch, and I know there's going to be no holding back on my part.

She doesn't get to have all the fun in her fantasies.

I reach out and pull her onto me, her warmth

melding with mine, igniting a fire that nearly consumes me. As I stare at her angelic face, I know I'm so fucked, but I can't find a reason to care any longer.

Her eyes flutter open, a small crease forming between them. "Luca?" Her voice, gravelly and enticing, heightens my arousal.

"You were dreaming about me," I say as a statement rather than a question.

"A much nicer version of you," she replies, and I can't help but grin.

"Is that what you dream of, Raven?" My hands slide over her ass, pressing her closer until she gasps. "A *nicer* me?"

Just when I think I have her right where I want her, she tries to roll over. "One who doesn't treat me like shit would do."

My hold tightens until I'm certain she can't go anywhere. "It wasn't my intention to dismiss you earlier." My words have her eyes widening.

"Then what were you trying to do?" she challenges.

"To not burn the world for trying to take you from me," I say earnestly. "It's not easy accepting you into my life, Raven. If I do, I won't be able to lose you. Not without consequences that will shake the foundations of this town to its core."

She doesn't look the least bit scared, which turns me on even more. "What would you do if you lost me?"

Her question makes my body shake with a soft chuckle. Her pleasure seems to thrive on my potential rage, another unexpected aspect of this woman.

My fingers trail lightly over her back until her skin pebbles beneath my touch. "I would kill anyone connected to you being taken from me. I would burn buildings. I would terrorize the streets. I would bring Hell to Earth."

"All for me?" she asks quietly, pausing briefly. "Why?"

I know if I utter the words that she deserves to hear, there will be no going back. This will be me admitting that from the moment I laid eyes on this woman, I knew I was done for. I thought if I could pretend that wasn't the case, I could stop it from happening.

Yet, as I gaze into her intoxicating eyes, I know the risk will be worth the reward.

"Because you're everything I'm not, Raven," I say. "I saw a light in your eyes the moment you stepped onto that stage that I longed to lose myself in. The innocence you radiated that I never had the chance of knowing myself while growing up in the family that I did. In those first few seconds, you made me want things I had forbidden myself from desiring. A life where I could simply be a man who desires a woman without questioning why it would be wrong for both of us."

Her eyes glaze over, her lips parting, but no words escape. She leans forward, attempting to kiss me, but my instinctive reaction is to turn my head, severing any momentum we might have just gained.

Olivia pushes at my chest, struggling to free herself of me, but I refuse to let her go. "You have no idea how difficult this is for me."

My words are a plea for her to understand. To know that staying here, accepting me, won't be easy, but that just maybe it might be worth it if she can be patient.

"Why won't you kiss me?" she demands, eyes narrowed and searching mine.

I have no answer for her. It's just not something I've done. Not since I was a rowdy teenager. Kissing always led to feelings, and those feelings led to rage, and rage made me...

"Maintaining control is something I've always had to fight for," I finally say, because it's the best explanation I can offer. "I can't lose control with you, Raven. You're far too precious for that."

"Damn you," she mutters, closing her eyes and leaning her forehead against my chest.

I release her, not wanting to cause her further pain, but as I try to move her back to the mattress, she presses her weight down, anchoring herself to me.

"You can go back—"

She easily cuts me off. "No, I can't. Not after all that. Not when you make me question everything I thought I believed. Not when I know I should, but my body won't be able to rest until you've satisfied it. I can't go back to anything. Not now."

There's a tinge of pain to her words that has me continuing to try to push her away. "I can find somewhere else for you to stay that will be just as safe."

Her head shakes, and a smile plays at the edges of her mouth. "You don't understand."

I open my mouth to ask her what I couldn't possibly

understand, but she shocks the hell out of me by grinding her hips over my cock.

"No more talking. Just...shut the fuck up and put your dick in me."

I know I don't deserve her, but that doesn't stop me from claiming her as she demands. I yank her sleep shorts to the side as I lift her hips up and reach between us. She's already wet for me, which loosens the tightening in my chest where a part of me wonders if maybe this isn't what she truly wants. That maybe she only allows me to touch her because my wanting her is what keeps her safe.

If only I wasn't a selfish bastard and could tell her that even if she rejected me, I still wouldn't let anyone else place a single finger on her ivory skin.

Olivia lifts her hips, and I hastily shove my briefs down just enough to free myself. As she slides down over my cock, the moan that escapes from between her lips nearly makes me come right then and there.

"So much better than my dreams," she murmurs as she sits up and rocks herself over me.

My hands clutch her pajamas, frustrated that I can't feel all of her. Instead of wasting time to properly remove the clothing, I reach for each of the seams on the side of her shorts and tear them apart. The sound reverberates through the quiet room, eliciting a grin from Olivia's face as I toss the shredded cotton to the side.

She lifts her shirt and reveals her glorious tits for me. I reach up and squeeze them as she starts moving again. Allowing her to take the lead for the moment, she grinds over me without a care in the world. Her hands reach up and tangle with her long locks, taking from me whatever she needs.

I thrust upward, matching her intensity and giving just as much as she wants to take. Her heated skin trembles under my touch as her cries get louder, urging me on. Pinching both of her nipples, I savor the gasp that escapes her lips, tugging her forward until I can capture one of them in my mouth. I suck hard, relishing the way she screams my name.

After repeating the action with the other, I can't stand allowing her to be on top any longer. I reverse our roles with a rumble in my chest.

Her legs entwine with mine as I pin her down, guiding her hands above her head. Keeping my eyes locked with hers, I surge forward, each thrust increasing in pressure. Her cheeks flush with crimson as her breathing becomes rapid and her back arches, pushing her closer to me, deepening my movements.

I pound into her, not stopping even as her moans of pleasure increase and her pussy tightens around my cock. I take everything she's willing to give and then some, aware that I'm a selfish bastard who can't change his nature.

Not now. Not when she needs me to be the cold-blooded killer that she met that night in the alleyway. Even if she doesn't realize it or know the ruthless truths that I've tried to withhold from her.

Shivers ripple through my spine, building until they reach an apex. The speed with which I own her body accelerates, and I revel in the way she melts beneath me, reaching her climax for the second time as I find my own release.

Fuck. Being with her shouldn't feel so damn good.

It's a recipe for disaster, but I don't care. Or don't want to. Not right now.

I brush away the hair that's stuck to her glistening forehead and stare down at her. "You need to understand that I'm going to piss you off again. I won't always show you the respect you deserve or give you what you want. But I need you to know that it's not because I don't care, Raven. Can you handle that?"

Without missing a beat, she nods. "I can. For now."

Those last two words send a jolt of fear through me, a kind I've never experienced before. "For now" might not be enough for me, but if she can accept me as I am, then I'll deal with it. For now.

23

OLIVIA

With the remnants of sleep still clinging to me, I anticipate exhaustion to weigh me down this morning. Yet, my mind buzzes with an electric energy that refuses to let me settle.

The words Luca uttered last night, and the intense actions that followed... I initially dismissed them as figments of my addled brain—a vivid and overwhelming fantasy. Yet, when he left this morning, assumingly to work, he gently brushed the back of his hand over my cheek as I still lay in bed, promising me that he'd do his best to be back in time to have dinner with me.

Since that moment, I've showered, dressed, and spent too much time straightening my hair, then curling it, only to straighten it again. All that was followed by dusting surfaces in Luca's room that are already pristine, then moving shit around before putting it back where I found it.

I wanted to be angry with him after the way he

treated me. I had zero intentions of putting up with his hot and cold tendencies. I even swore to myself that I wouldn't think with my vagina any longer.

But then he opened his stupid mouth and spoke those even stupider words that weren't at all stupid, effectively turning me into putty for him to do what he pleases with.

The heartache in his eyes when he explained not kissing me because he was afraid to lose control nearly brought tears to my eyes. I know nothing of his childhood —he's never even mentioned his parents outside of saying that his dad built this place—but I try to put myself in his shoes. It's likely that from the moment he was old enough to hold a gun, he was being groomed for the life of a mafia king.

It's sad to imagine Luca's child-self growing up like that, but by knowing a bit more about who he is now, I can at least sympathize. He practically begged me to accept what he can give and let it be enough. Against my better judgment, I granted him that favor, even if it meant sacrificing my own desires.

That might end up being a mistake, but as my thoughts continue to race, I try to believe otherwise.

When I'm halfway through rearranging the books on the shelf by color, Justine sweeps into the room with the biggest grin on her face, her auburn hair floating around her shoulders as she moves forward, engulfing me in an unexpected hug.

"Last night was absolutely incredible," she squeals, her excitement palpable. "The things Jaxon does to me...

You have to give in to Luca and experience how amazing this mafia life can be."

I shake my head and try to hide my own blush. If only she knew...

Her fingers grip my shoulder when I attempt to turn back to the bookshelf. "Olivia Danes, what have you been keeping from me?"

"Nothing," I mutter, but she doesn't relent.

"If you don't tell me what's happened, I'm going to...I don't know, but something and you're not going to like it."

I chuckle as she narrows her eyes, her determination unwavering. "That's quite the threat," I say. "But I don't kiss and tell."

Well, it's not as if we kissed, but she doesn't need to know that. I feel like that would shatter what little trust Luca has given me. Even if he never found out, I would know.

Justine glares at me with accusatory eyes. "You totally fucked him, didn't you?"

"I'm not justifying that question with an answer," I say with a straight face.

"Ha!" she practically shouts, releasing me. "That's all the answer I need." She leans and lowers her voice. "With his quiet yet deadly demeanor, I've always imagined him as an animal in bed. Please, tell me I'm right."

This woman has no boundaries, but I can't find it in me to be annoyed or deny her as I whisper, "Ravenous is more accurate."

"I fucking knew it!" Her fist shoots up into the air and

she gives me a wicked grin. "You're totally staying here. I just knew it the moment I saw you. One look at you with your pants down and there was no other option except to make you my best friend."

Only now does it occur to me that Justine, having chosen to remain with Jaxon, has likely faced more life-altering changes than most would find comfortable. I've already been keeping Tori in the dark, and I haven't even bothered to respond to Sandi.

Have I already made the same choice as Justine without realizing it?

The thought churns my stomach. I don't want to sacrifice my identity for a man, but in the same breath, I wonder if perhaps that's not entirely true. Maybe I'm simply evolving into a version of myself that had always been waiting to emerge, hidden beneath the surface until this chaotic world forced me to confront it.

I don't have the answers, and for now, I choose not to dwell on the uncertainty. I'm confined to this compound, and I'll make the most of it while I can.

"I'm heading down to the gym," Justine announces, thankfully shifting away from the topic of our sex lives. "Care to join me?"

Considering my sleep-deprived state, I shake my head. "Count me in for tomorrow, though."

Her eyebrows wiggle mischievously. "Too sore from all that action? Don't worry, you'll acclimate soon enough."

I cough, seemingly choking on air, thanks to her lack of filter. "Right. Okay."

She hugs me again. "You can't fight this. I'll break you down eventually."

When I pull back, I don't quite release her. "Being your friend requires no breaking down for me. I promise you that."

Justine blows me a kiss as she makes her way back out the door. "Good, because I'm pretty fucking awesome."

That she is, and it's only because of her awesomeness that I've lasted this long staying here.

I try to go back to organizing the books once she's gone, but I'm already bored of that and consider changing my mind and meeting Justine in the gym. Before I make my decision, I head toward the window by the table and push aside the curtains.

The sky is clear, and it's then that I realize—thanks to my forced captivity—I haven't been under the sun's rays in weeks. *What the fuck?* No wonder my emotions have been all over the place. I've been getting the wrong kind of vitamin D.

Well, maybe not wrong, but...

I flip the lock on the window and, as I reach for the bottom to yank it up, a steel shutter races down from the top, nearly taking my hands off with its force.

"Mother fuck," I growl into the empty room. Then, one by one, the other windows do the same thing. "Luca."

I'm moving to my phone before it rings, and when I see his name on the screen, unsurprised that he's already programmed in there, I answer with a snarl. "What the hell was that?"

"A security measure," he answers hastily. "You're okay?"

"No, I'm not fucking okay," I snap. My hands tremble slightly, the adrenaline from the close call still coursing through my veins. "I almost just lost both of my hands. Don't you think that's something you should have warned me about?"

Luca's admission comes with a tinge of remorse. "I didn't when you first came to my room, but yes, I probably should have by now," he concedes. "Also, don't try to disengage the lock on the front door without the code. You'll get electrocuted."

My eyes widen, and if he were standing in front of me, my fist would be itching to connect with his face. Okay, maybe not literally, but the desire to do so is palpable.

"What were you trying to do?" he probes, likely sensing my rising ire.

I release a heavy sigh, trying to gather my thoughts and temper my emotions. "I was just trying to get some fresh air, maybe feel the sun on my skin," I explain, my voice tinged with a touch of exasperation. "Do you realize I haven't been outside except for that night at the club? And I'm not even counting that occurrence since the sun wasn't out."

"You never asked about going outside," he states simply, devoid of accusation.

"You told me I couldn't leave without the risk of being killed," I counter, my frustration boiling over.

"Having at least some sense of self-perseveration, why the hell would I ask?"

He's quiet for a moment. "I was going to show you myself, but there's a garden you can go visit while still remaining within the compound walls."

It's quite possible that I would choke him if he was standing in front of me at this point. "Where?"

"It's on the second floor," he explains, as if this isn't a big deal when the only things I've been drawing have been flowers. Maybe telling me about the garden the moment I was allowed to leave the room *might* have been a good idea.

Fucking men.

After taking another deep breath, I ask, "And are there any other security measures I need to be aware of?"

He chuckles. "No, Raven. You're safe within the rest of the compound."

"Are you *laughing* at me?" I ask incredulously.

"Not at all," he promises. "I merely enjoy the way you speak to me."

My foot taps on the hard floor. "Like I said when you *kidnapped* me, you need new friends. Ones who don't kiss your ass."

"I'll take that into advisement," he says, clearly placating me. "Enjoy the garden for as long as you like. I'll find you there when I'm done if you're not in the room."

Annoyed with all the things, I don't bother to say my goodbyes. I end the call and return to the bedroom to grab my sketch pad that I left on the dresser. Maybe I won't want to punch him by the time he returns if I get some drawing in.

Once I have my stuff together, I cautiously exit the apartment, eyeing the door a little closer now that I know it can electrocute me. That really would have been something to tell me before. It's only now occurring to me that ever since he told me I was allowed to leave the apartment, the door hasn't once been locked.

I make my way to the second floor, one I've yet to visit, and once the doors open, I realize I still don't know where I'm supposed to go. Glancing left, then right, I head toward the right hallway. When I round the first corner, I slam into a hard chest, gasping as my stuff tumbles to the ground.

"I'm so sorry," I quickly stammer and bend to grab my things without looking up.

A heavy hand snags my wrist. "Let me help."

His voice is oddly familiar, but I can't place where I recognize it from until he stands back up, meeting my curious gaze. It's one of the men from the first night in the SUV, the guy with the scar on his face.

He's not as menacing in the light—or maybe I'm just not as terrified. Either way, I smile at him. "Thanks. Do you know where the garden is by chance?"

He points behind me. "Back that way, second door on the right once you turn left."

"Thanks. Again."

He doesn't say anything else as I turn, which doesn't surprise me. It seems most of the men around here are fond of fewer words spoken.

I follow his directions and, within another minute, push open the door to the outside world. I inhale deeply and close my eyes, soaking up the moment. "Oh, I've missed this."

Funny the little things we take for granted. It isn't until they're gone that it's easy to understand how much something so simple as stepping outside can mean. This time, thankfully, it isn't too late for me to appreciate the value I hold for nature.

As I open my eyes, my gaze sweeps across the enclosure, which resembles more of a balcony than an actual garden, surrounded by towering brick walls adorned with menacing barbed wire. But it's not the imposing security measures that leave me speechless; it's the breathtaking sight of the array of vibrant flowers that stretches out before me. It extinguishes any and all frustration I just had with Luca.

Peonies, their lush blooms unfurling in delicate shades of pink and white, captivate my attention. Dahlias stand tall and proud, displaying an assortment of bold hues that range from fiery oranges to rich purples. Lilies, their petals elegantly curved, emit a subtle fragrance that lingers in the air. Clusters of carnations, with their ruffled petals, burst forth in a riot of colors, creating a kaleidoscope that mimics the liveliness I've been missing in my sketches.

Overwhelmed by the beauty surrounding me, I take hesitant steps forward, my fingers outstretched. I allow my hand to graze the velvety softness of the petals as I wander along the narrow path. Each touch evokes a sense of wonder, as if I am caressing nature's own artwork.

Inhaling deeply, I'm instantly intoxicated by the symphony of scents that envelops me. The sweet fragrance of peonies pairs playfully with the earthy aroma of dahlias. The delicate perfume of lilies mingles with the spicy, clove-like scent of carnations.

As I stroll deeper into the garden, the sun shines down on me, for the moment unobstructed by the towering walls and casting a warm and gentle glow over my skin. Its warmth embraces me and brings a certain rejuvenation that I've been missing over the passing weeks by being trapped indoors.

The tension and worries that clung to me moments ago dissolve, replaced by a serene calmness that I haven't felt in much too long. I take a deep breath, filling my lungs with the pure, crisp air. With each exhale, I release any remnants of stress, choosing to savor this moment.

A gentle smile graces my lips as I reach for my phone, sending Luca a thank you I intend to expand on later once he's home. His reply is swift.

Luca: Did you find the cabinet on the back wall?

My eyes scan the area, and I spot the storage space that I had missed before. Crossing the tranquil garden, anticipation builds within me as I open the wooden doors.

Tears prick at my eyes, and my throat tightens with emotions I struggle to contain. Inside the cabinet, two shelves hold an assortment of painting materials and an easel with dozens of blank canvases stacked beneath it.

On the stand is an unsigned note:

Make as big of a mess as you want. This space is yours.

Damn him. Damn him for being kind when I least expect it.

Me: Thank you isn't sufficient, but that's all I have right now.

Luca: Leaving you speechless is more than enough. Enjoy, Raven.

Oh, I fully intend to, but even better is that it no longer matters to me if Luca can kiss me or not. Between knowing that he took care of everything when it came to my house and paying the debts my mother owed, then giving me this perfect space, I have all the proof I need to know that he's worth hanging around for.

The mafia be damned.

24

LUCA

I would have preferred to witness Olivia's reaction to the garden firsthand, but her silent awe will have to suffice until I can join her later. Right now, I have a pain in my ass to finally remove.

Jaxon's been working every angle we have to find Titan Moretti. Thanks to a tip from one of our inside men at the FBI, we're headed toward a location just over the state line, crossing into Washington.

If this piece of shit thinks he can continue to fuck with my life, he's sorely mistaken. If he'd stopped with killing the senator, I might have let him get away by merely disappearing, but since then, he's continued to poke at my business, which I don't take well.

Between the whispered lies to my board members and the threats against Olivia, I've had enough. More than enough, in fact. I'll be killing this man with my own hands. Hell, maybe I'll even stuff his head and hang it in my office at home.

The idea has merit, but it's dashed away when I realize we're pulling up to the house where we've been told Titan is holed up at. It's still daylight, and I don't normally like to make noise when it's easier for people to see who's doing the shooting versus who's left for dead, but I don't have the patience to sit on this information until tonight. Especially when I already have plans.

Jaxon glances at me from the driver's seat as he parks two houses down from our target. "Damon and his team are already positioned in the backyard," he announces, gesturing toward Aaron and Ethan in the back. "These two will flank us, and then we'll breach the door before moving in."

The plan is just how I would have made it myself, but after so many years working with Jaxon, it's no different when he makes them on my behalf.

I tug at the bulletproof vest under my dress shirt. They're not my favorite to wear, but I'm also fully aware that I'm not invincible and I'll be damned if a bullet takes me out.

"Fuck," Jaxon mutters right after his phone pings with a new message. When his stare meets mine, I already know I'm not going to like what he has to say. "The bounty for Olivia was just upped to a quarter mil."

I swallow my anger, aware that losing control now will only hinder our mission. The bounty will soon become inconsequential when there's no one left to pay it.

With a steadying breath, I look toward the house we'll be breaking into, forcing myself back into the right state of mind. "Can Damon get a read on how many bodies are inside?"

"He counts twelve in total," Jaxon answers, and I grin.

This is going to be almost too easy. "Let's go then."

I tighten the silencer to my forty caliber Smith and Wesson, holding the black grip in my right hand as I double-check the safety is off and make sure the mag is filled with all twenty rounds. Once I'm out of the SUV, I reach into the glove box for two extra mags to keep in my back pockets. Sixty bullets should be enough to lead the way with only twelve maggots to dispose of.

Once we're all outside the vehicle, I glance around and realize someone is missing—a familiar face I'm accustomed to having in my crew for moments like this. "Where's Vin?"

"He stayed back at the house," Jaxon replies. "I assigned him to oversee the others there, just in case."

It's another decision for which I'm grateful Jaxon took the lead.

With a cautious scan of the quiet neighborhood, I silently hope most people are either at work or mindlessly glued to their televisions, unaware of the impending bloodshed. The last thing we need is the police showing up, allowing Titan to slip away.

We navigate toward the house, its innocuous white siding and navy-blue shutters projecting a facade of normalcy that Titan has likely never known. But his lies are about to be exposed.

Silently, we move around the concealing bushes, then

make a swift dash toward the porch as soon as the foliage ends. Within seconds, my foot crashes through the door, sending wooden splinters flying, and the first suppressed shots echo from my gun's muzzle.

Men take cover behind couches and tables, but nothing is going to keep them safe from me. Well, nothing other than information that might prove useful.

Jaxon stays at my side as Aaron and Ethan keep to our left and right. The door is shoved closed by one of them, and we move further into the house.

An adversary stands before us, brandishing a knife. As he releases it into the air, Jaxon's gunfire rings out, two rounds finding their mark in the idiot's skull. However, he manages a final act of defiance.

The knife slices into Jaxon's left arm, and he retreats behind me, extracting the blade. "Stupid mother fucker," he hisses. "I'll kill him again for making me bleed."

My oldest friend doesn't like to lose. Though, once the threat is over, I find enjoyment in his displeasure.

I catch a brief glimpse of movement from the hallway on my right and ready my pistol. As soon as there's another shadow, I pull the trigger back and grin when the sound of someone dropping to the ground echoes.

"Be the first person to tell me where Moretti is, and you might have a chance to live," I assert, my gun steady and my body primed to react in case more blades come hurtling our way.

A hand extends from behind the wall, pointing toward the kitchen on our left. "There's a room back there. If he's still here, that's where he'll be."

Well, that was almost disappointingly easy. I signal to Aaron and Ethan to restrain those who aren't already dead. If they're so willing to cooperate, we might as well keep them for the time being.

Jaxon is back on his feet and joining me as I walk toward the kitchen. My eyes cast a glance at his arm, but he already has the wound covered with a strip of his shirt and doesn't seem to have a problem holding his gun up.

"Barely stuck me," he says, but as we pass the man who got him, he still shoots him once more and kicks the corpse in the head for good measure.

I shake my head but keep my eyes forward. Titan isn't going to go easy, I'm certain of that. Keeping our guards up until he's dead is a necessity I won't dismiss.

As we enter the kitchen, I spot a white steel door just off the back. I wave Jaxon forward with one hand while keeping my pistol pointed forward with the other.

Jaxon tests the handle, but it's locked. Not that I really expected otherwise, but given the door is likely to be bulletproof, it's worth checking.

Even though we can't shoot through it, nobody can shoot at us, either.

Considering this, I use the butt of my gun to forcefully pound on the door. "Come out, Titan. There's nowhere else for you to go. Make things easy on yourself and surrender."

Seconds pass, but there's no response. Not even a sound from within the room. Either the door is soundproof, or Titan isn't hiding there.

"Blow it up," I decide, taking a step back. I lack the

patience to waste time attempting to open the door by other means. If Titan chooses to remain silent while hiding inside, then he can perish from the shrapnel for all I care.

"Ethan," Jaxon calls without turning around. "Bring me the Semtex."

I turn to see Ethan, the youngest member of our group, approaching. His black fatigues are pristine, devoid of any blood, and he wears a confident grin on his face as he hands Jaxon the explosive. "Three are tied up. The rest are dead or about to be since they ran out the back toward Damon."

"Keep watch," I command firmly. "More of them could be anywhere in this house."

"You got it, Boss." He drops the smile and nods before turning to go back to his post.

And that's why I keep him around. Young doesn't have to mean stupid. He's always compliant and a quick learner, which goes a long way in proving his worth to me.

Jaxon secures the Semtex to the door and puts a hand on my chest. "Might want to back up around the corner. It's designed to be precise, but the impact still packs a punch."

I don't question him as we step outside of the kitchen and cover our ears. With the press of a button on Jaxon's phone, the bomb goes off and the entire house shudders with the force. Cabinets across from us fall from the walls, and even the wood floor beneath our feet cracks.

My brow raises at him. "Maybe go a little smaller with the explosives next time."

"What's the fun in that?" he jokes as he moves around the corner, gun already at the ready.

I follow in his footsteps, narrowing my eyes to see through the dust that still billows in the destroyed kitchen.

The door is at least mutilated on the floor, which is the most important thing. Slowing, we're careful not to rush the room when we can't see too far in front of our faces.

"Fuck," Jaxon snarls. "There's a hole in the ground." I see him bend down. "One that wasn't caused by the Semtex."

That motherfucker. He got away. Again.

I can't comprehend how he keeps eluding me, but when I finally get my hands on him, he'll suffer more than any man has ever endured under my wrath. That much I guarantee.

"Bring me one of his idiots," I shout, stepping out of the destruction.

Ethan drags in the one with a bullet wound in his outer shoulder and tosses him at my feet. "He's the one with the flappy lips."

I bend down, grab the man by the back of his neck, and snarl. "If you want to keep those *lips* much longer, you better fucking tell me where he disappeared to."

His shit-brown eyes widen. "I've only worked for him a week. This is the only place I've been."

My frustration level has reached a new high, and I'm

about to stomp his head when he adds quieter, "The other guy. He's been here longer. Maybe I can get him to talk."

Fucking little rat. I hate men like him that would so easily turn on their own, but in this instance, I decide to go with it. Desperation doesn't feel good, but I can't deny that's where I'm at.

Desperate to get my hands around Moretti's neck.

I bring him closer, my voice deadly. "If you upset me one more time, it will be the last thing you do. Understand?"

He nods, and I shove him toward the ground. "Put him in Damon's SUV. I don't want to see his face again until he has something useful to say."

Ethan doesn't reply, but he picks up the rat and hauls him out the back door just as Damon comes in.

He glances around, and I can see his appreciation for the destruction, but his next words are filled with urgency. "We need to go. Someone called in a noise complaint."

"And you didn't see where Titan might have popped out at?" I ask, because that fucking tunnel has to lead somewhere.

Daman shakes his head. "But I'll come back once the police are done and find where it goes. Moretti won't get away for long."

No, he fucking wouldn't.

25

LUCA

It's hard to shake the fury still storming within me as Jaxon and I get back to the compound, but when I check the cameras to see where Olivia is and spot her still in the garden, painting as if the world isn't out to kill her...I find a way to quelch my rage.

I promised her dinner tonight, and I intend to follow through.

Without waiting for Jaxon, I step into the elevator and press the button for floor two. The doors start to close, but before they can seal, a hand pushes through.

When they reopen, Jaxon is on the other side with one raised brow. "In a hurry to get somewhere?"

I don't bother to answer him as he steps inside to join me.

"I know that didn't go as planned, but at least we have more leads," he says. I don't want his optimism right now, though. I want Titan's head on a spike.

It takes everything in me not to snarl at him. It's not

his fault that Titan has slipped through our grasp twice now and has upped the bounty on Olivia. I've tried not to think about it since Jaxon told me earlier, but something deeper about that move bothers me. It shouldn't be public knowledge that I've grown to care for her. She hasn't left the compound except that one night.

My mind searches my memory, wondering if I did anything to alert anyone to my desire for this woman, but hell, I didn't even console her after the attack. I let Justine handle that.

Why Titan thinks using her life as a way to throw me off is beyond me, but unfortunately, he isn't wrong. Which could also be why he's raised the bounty. We've gotten too close to him. If she meant nothing to me, I wouldn't be trying so hard to find him.

Jaxon still stands there, patiently waiting for me to respond as the elevator moves. I don't know what he wants me to say.

"I doubled the amount of guards outside the compound," he adds, and I cut a glare his way. "I know you didn't want to draw attention by doing so, but Moretti clearly has thought this through. I won't stand by and put the women here at risk. Olivia isn't the only one who could get hurt by all this."

He's not wrong, but still. This is one of those moments where I'm close to feeling out of control, and I don't like it one fucking bit.

"The extra guards are fine," I reply curtly. "Even bring some of them inside, making sure we have constant eyes on every floor and not just through the cameras. If you're not with Justine, I'd advise that she's not left alone, and I'll do the same with Olivia."

A grin tugs at the corner of Jaxon's mouth. "Did you know that as soon as Olivia's wrist was feeling better, they started training together? Those girls will give someone a run for their money."

"Until a gun is pulled out and a bullet goes through their skulls," I say harshly. "They shouldn't be left alone until we know this threat is over."

He sobers quickly. "Yes, Boss. What else can I do?"

"Get out of my way, so I can get where I'm going." I brush past him and walk out of the elevator that's now at floor two.

He reaches a hand toward me and grabs hold of my shoulder. "It's okay to care about her, Luc."

I don't turn back. I can't, because I don't agree. Even if that doesn't change my feelings toward Olivia, I know it's wrong of me to care for her. To have brought her into this world that she was blissfully unaware of just weeks ago, and now, she has no idea just how much her life is at risk.

Jaxon releases me, and the elevator closes. Once I'm alone, I take a deep inhale and steel my expression for greeting Olivia. She doesn't need bad news the moment I see her. After dinner will be soon enough.

My pace quickly takes me to the garden area I had revived specifically for her. Just a week ago, this place was filled with broken pots, dead plants, and weeds. After seeing how much she loved flowers and how respectful she was not to make a mess in the apartment, I knew she needed somewhere she didn't have to worry about such things and would also bring her a slice of comfort.

Something I know I'm not entirely capable of.

I can protect her, and I can fuck her unlike anyone else ever will, but that doesn't mean I'm good for her. That she won't get hurt again because of me.

My palm presses against the door. Not yet. I can't lose focus yet.

With another deep breath, I enter the garden and see Olivia sitting in front of the easel, her back to me.

In front of her is the monstrous brick wall that keeps intruders out, but above her is a stunning sunset, filled with an array of orange, purple, and red colors that she has no issues capturing on the canvas before her.

Quietly, I move closer to her, observing the fluid brush strokes and as she carefully chooses the next hue to place on the art.

Next to her are several other paintings that she's already completed, all varying versions of the flowers within this very garden.

My eyes make their way back to my raven who still has no idea I'm here. Her hair is up in a messy bun. She's wearing one of my white t-shirts and jean shorts that are frayed at the ends. Her feet are bare, and she hums quietly, completely lost in her own little world.

Fuck.

Seeing her this way twists my chest, and I'm not sure if it's a good thing or not, but I know I can't keep my hands to myself a moment longer.

My fingers brush over her heated skin from being out in the sun all afternoon, but I obviously didn't think my actions through, because she swings a fist back, still holding the paintbrush, and punches me in the jaw while also getting maroon paint all over my suit.

Apparently, Jaxon wasn't wrong. Olivia has been practicing.

I rub the sore spot on my face and shake my head at her. She's frozen in place, her mouth open in surprise and eyes wide, but that only lasts for a moment before she starts laughing. She reaches out, swiping her thumb over my cheek. "If you're going to have paint on you, the blending should at least be right."

The smirk on her face has me forgetting every bad thing that's happened today. Once again, she's enthralled me by not being afraid of my wrath. Little does she know that by doing so, it also takes away my rage.

I steal the brush from her hand, smearing the same color across her cheek. "Seems only fair for you to match."

Her brows raise. "Only fair, huh?" She slides her hand down the front of my suit. "Only fair should include reminding you that it's okay to have a little chaos in your life."

I have too much of that and don't need anymore, but a mess in the form of this woman isn't something I'm going to shy away from.

My hands reach for the button of her shorts and pop them open. "How about a little body painting?"

Her cheeks flush and the excitement in her eyes is

undeniable. "I think that's probably my favorite fantasy ever."

I lean closer, pressing my lips to her ear and whisper, "Then, allow me to make it come true."

Reaching behind her, I dip my fingers into the nearest colors of purple and blue before bringing my hand back. With my other hand, I yank the shirt from her body before slowly gliding my fingertips over the swell of her chest.

"Something like this?" I ask.

Her breathing shutters. "Something like that."

My touch leaves a trail of mixing colors and moves further south. With a swift tug, her shorts are at her ankles and I'm reaching for more paint. This time, I coat my palms, already knowing where I want to leave my mark.

She stays ever so still as I move around her. With my lips against her neck, I nip at her heated skin and smack my palms over her ass cheeks.

Her body flinches as she mutters, "Fuck me."

"Stay still and have some patience, Raven." I grab one of the blank canvases and set it on her vacated chair. She still has her back to me as I lift her up, setting her freshly painted ass onto the white background.

"Oh my God," she gasps. "Did you just make a painting with my ass?"

My grip moves to her thighs as I press her down onto the canvas. "No. I *started* a painting."

It won't be complete until I have an impression of her tits on there as well.

"Stand," I instruct as I find more colors. A little green and silver should pair nicely with the purple and blue already present. Bringing the tubes instead of using the samplings she already has out, I squirt the first over her left tit, then reach behind her and unclasp her bra.

"What are you doing, Luca Monroe?" she questions with a tone of seriousness, yet there's a glimmer in her eyes that only continues to intensify as I have my fun.

"Making myself something." Once her tits are free, I smear the already present silver over her nipple, then do the same with the green on the other. "Don't move."

She barely breathes as I turn around for the canvas, lifting it up and pressing it to her chest. She leans in, but that's not enough pressure to give me the details I desire. With one arm, I hold her tightly against me, the canvas locked between us.

"You're something I didn't expect," she admits as I stare down at her oval face.

"Then, I guess that makes us even in that regard," I reply before releasing her and taking in my artwork. The colors are all smeared together, there are lumps of paint in certain places, and nothing *blends* as she often likes to talk about.

To anyone else, this would appear to be the work of a toddler, but to me, I can make out every curve and dimple, and it's perfect.

"Mind if I add something?" Olivia says, gazing at the canvas next to me.

"As long as you don't touch what's already there, by all means."

She takes the painting from me and places it on the easel before picking up the previously discarded paint brush from the ground. With her ass in the air, still covered in plenty of paint, I don't miss the opportunity to smack her colored cheeks.

She merely laughs at my antics before dipping the brush into shimmering seafoam. She brings the brush closer to the canvas, then covers the brush with her fingertip before forcing it back and flicking the paint over the art.

It doesn't take away from what's already there, but as she moves around, filling in blank spaces, her gentle touch does complete the painting in a way I don't expect. Something about that feels more like a metaphor I don't want to think too hard about. I'll leave that for another day.

When she turns back to me with the biggest of smiles on her face, I know I can't wait any longer to sink my cock into her. Only bothering with my pants, I undo my belt and shove them down just far enough to free myself.

Without missing a beat, Olivia jumps into my arms and wraps her legs around my waist as I walk us to the bench between some of the planters. As soon as we're sitting, she lifts up and grabs my dick like she owns it and lines herself up before dropping her head back, lowering her pulsing pussy right where it belongs.

"This isn't going to take much after that," she says breathily.

That's not a problem for me. At least, not right now. I can take my time with her later when we're somewhere I don't need to concern myself with someone interrupting us and laying eyes on what's only meant for me.

She bounces above me, slamming herself over my cock with little guidance from me and her head still pointed at the sky.

I grip her tits, pinching both nipples and smearing more paint between the two of us until she cries out, digging her nails into my thighs where she's anchored herself.

My upper body leans forward, one arm wrapping around her waist as my mouth finds her neck, biting down hard enough to leave a mark. Her body tenses, but the groan that comes next, followed by the tightening of her pussy, tells me this woman likes things a little rough.

"So close," she murmurs, and I know I want to come when she does, so I join in her efforts, lifting my hips in time with hers.

It's not exactly enough, but she seems to understand what I need without me saying anything, because one of her hands snakes past my slacks that are still at mid-thigh and gives my balls a gentle squeeze.

The unexpected touch sends a jolt of pleasure through me and has rumbles echoing from my chest. She continues with her touch, growing firmer in pressure with each passing second, and within a minute we're both fully sated and collapsing into each other's arms.

She chuckles against my shoulder, and even though I can't see her face, I can hear the smile in her words. "That's one hell of a greeting. And here I thought I was going to be thanking *you* for the garden."

My hands tightly grip her ass. "Don't worry. The night is still young. There's still plenty of time for you to get on your knees and thank me properly."

Her pussy tightens over my dick, and I smirk. It's about fucking time I claim her mouth.

26

OLIVIA

Getting back to the apartment, both Luca and I covered in paint and doing my best not to leave any marks in our trail, isn't an easy feat, but we manage for the most part, and the first place I head is the shower. I expect Luca to join me after he orders dinner so I can properly thank him for the garden, but as the minutes tick by, my stomach begins to churn.

As soon as all the paint has been scrubbed from my body and hair, I'm out of the shower and rushing into the bedroom, still dripping with water even though the towel is wrapped around me.

Luca is talking on the phone and pacing the room. His voice is low, and his shoulders are tight with tension. I can't make out the words he's saying with how far away he is, but I already know something is wrong.

He spots me and seems to hang up the phone as he demands, "You need to get dressed."

I follow him toward the closet where he's heading instead of doing as I'm told. "Why? What's wrong?"

"People are trying to break into the compound," he says sharply. "I need to go make sure that doesn't happen, but you need to be ready to leave in case it does."

Fear swells inside me, and I freeze, standing in his way as he attempts to change his clothes. He grabs my shoulders and squeezes hard. "I need you to do as I say, Raven. Right the fuck now."

His words pierce through my fog, but I still don't move. "Why are people breaking in?"

Luca briefly closes his eyes as he takes a deep breath. "There's a bounty on you. They're here to collect."

One would think that seeing a dead senator, being shot at, then locked in an underground cell, followed by someone trying to violate me and possibly kill me would be the worst kind of terror I could be consumed with. Yet, hearing those words leave Luca's lips, knowing that the threat on my life is more than real, it's right here at the compound...has spots flickering at the edge of my vision and me ready to pass out.

Luca grips my chin between his fingers and lifts my face up toward his. I think he's going to yell at me for not listening still, but he surprises me by roughly placing his lips on my forehead. "I need to know that you're going to be okay if I leave this room, Raven. Can you get dressed and be ready to run if I tell you to? Can you do that for me?"

Mother fuck fuck.

I want to tell him no and beg him not to leave me, but I don't. Instead, I force myself to nod and step away from him. "I'll be fine. I promise."

I'm not entirely sure that's true, but what I do know is that the longer Luca is up here with me, the more likely whoever is trying to break in is going to succeed. I need him to do what he does best while I figure out a way to keep my shit together.

He goes back to grabbing what he needs from his closet, and I go to my dresser, dropping my towel and moving on autopilot as I select jeans, socks, underwear, and a plain black tee to wear.

By the time I have everything but the shirt on, Luca is already dressed in black cargo pants with a white t-shirt underneath a bulletproof vest and a gun at his hip, secured in a holster.

I swallow hard. This is actually fucking happening. This is real life right now. The moment in the garden, the peace I lost myself to all afternoon, that was fiction. A lie to make the reality more manageable. In this moment, nothing is *manageable*.

Luca grips the back of my neck tightly. "You won't leave this room. The door will be locked, and the shock factor I told you about earlier? That will be on," he warns, staring hard into my frightened eyes. "The shutters are still down from earlier and nothing will penetrate them. You're safe in here, Raven."

Those last words seem like more of a reassurance for him rather than me.

"But I still need to be ready to run?" I ask, because that seems rather important to know before he leaves.

"Yes," he replies as his phone vibrates loudly in his pocket. "Justine isn't home, or she'd be here with you. I'll get you out of here just as soon as I can do so safely. I promise."

I nod and try to stay strong since that seems to be what he needs to see before he rushes out of here.

With one more look at me, he finally tears himself away and storms toward the front door. I watch from the bedroom as he jerks on the door, then glances back one last time.

There's no shared smile between us, no kisses blown to one another, no whispers of further promises. The hard lines of his face instead remind me of how serious this situation has quickly become, and when he slams the door shut and I hear the lock engage, I run back for the room to finish dressing so I can do as I've told him I would: be ready to run.

It only takes three minutes for me to finish, including putting on proper shoes and twisting my wet hair into a bun so that it's not a hazard, given I don't want to waste time doing anything else with it.

When I enter the living room where I've left not only my phone, but the painting Luca made, I try not to scream in frustration at the turn of events. I grab my phone and see more than a dozen missed calls and texts from Justine.

I call her back as I stand by the bar, staring at the door

that I'm not allowed to touch. "Fuck, Olivia. Answer your damn phone when there are people trying to kill you."

Justine's loud words boom through the speaker and right into my ear. "I was busy being told what to do."

"Where are you?" she asks hurriedly.

"In Luca's apartment," I reply, glancing around as I explain. "He told me to stay here. The steel shutters on the windows are all down, and he has the electricity on that fancy door of his turned on."

She breathes heavily, but it's not the sound of relief I'm hoping for. "Did he leave you with a gun?"

"Uh, no." Not that I'm against them—I've even shot several of them when I was growing up, thanks to Tori's dad inviting me to learn when she did—but I'm not sure I'd know what to do with one now.

"Go to Luca's closet," Justine says, then a video request comes through that I promptly answer before she can yell at me some more. When her face comes into view, I can tell she's at the shopping center with all the stores behind her, but I don't get to ask why before she's directing me again. "Turn the camera around so I can see the closet."

I do so, then turn on the light. "What now?"

"This is just like Jaxon's," she says, then points in the screen. "Open those drawers on the right. One or more of them should have guns, assuming Luca didn't take them all with him."

I only saw the one at his hip when he left, but that doesn't mean more weren't hidden in pockets.

It isn't until the third drawer that I find a silver pistol with two already-filled magazines lying next to it. "Take those, put one mag in, cock the gun, and put the other mag in your front pocket. It will be harder to lose that way if you're running."

Damn it. Her words aren't making me feel any better. "Have you had this happen to you before?"

"No, but that doesn't mean Jaxon hasn't prepared me," she answers. "Now, it's my turn to prepare you. Go back to the living room and, Olivia? Shoot any fucker who makes it past that door that isn't supposed to. Remember, it's your life or theirs. Don't choose them over yourself."

Her words weigh heavily on me, setting in the harsh reality that there's a chance I'll have to kill someone today. That I'll be responsible for taking their life.

The thought presses down on me, but the idea of doing so, of protecting myself no matter the cost, doesn't scare me as much as I expect. I wanted to kill Abel for hurting me in that nightclub. I can have that same feeling for anyone else who tries to lay a hand on me.

Not only can I, but I know I must.

"I need to go," she hurries. "I'm getting picked up by Ethan and Aaron and taken to who knows where, but I'm sure you'll end up there, too. Just be safe."

"I will and you, too," I reply, and feel like there should be more to say, but the screen goes dark before I can form the words.

With the gun heavy in my palm and the extra mag in

my pocket as instructed, I sit on the couch this time, eyes trained on the door and my phone in front of me on the table.

I can do this. These fuckers won't get me. At least, not easily.

27

LUCA

Leaving Olivia has a vice around my chest that serves as a constant reminder of what's at stake if anyone succeeds in breaking into the compound and getting close to her.

I rush downstairs and meet Jaxon in the main living room where Vin, Markus, and Jake are already waiting with him.

"Where are they trying to enter at?" I ask when I've barely stepped into the room.

"Where *aren't* they is a better question," Vin retorts, but shuts his mouth when both Jaxon and I cut him a glare.

He's been around since before I was in charge but hasn't seemed to learn when to keep his thoughts to himself.

Jaxon finally answers me. "They came in through the garage and somehow turned off nearly every camera and electrical wire we have on the outside to keep anyone from scaling the walls."

Fuck. They could have gotten to me and Olivia when we'd been in the garden. Or even before I arrived.

Knowing that I could have found her mutilated body instead of seeing her painting when I came back is more than enough to have me shaking with the need to kill.

"Where are our men set up, and where are our weak points?" I ask, knowing with this sort of surprise attack, there wouldn't have been enough of my guys around to secure the whole compound, even with the extra security.

Jaxon points toward the south then west of the building. "The front and garage are the most covered. We need more of us to push to the north and east."

I pull my gun from its holster and squeeze the handle firmly in my palm. "Then, let's fucking go."

The five of us split into two groups, Jaxon coming with me toward the north side of the compound while Vin, Markus, and Jake go east.

My feet increase in speed, and it's only seconds before I'm running through the hallways, glad to see all the steel shutters have been triggered. A fail safe I had installed years ago. One of many, but it doesn't seem as if most of the others are working.

"Do you think one of our men turned on us?" I ask Jaxon as our pace slows and we both walk cautiously with our guns lifted. "Titan has eluded us twice, and nobody should have figured out where *all* of our cameras and wires are. Not at least without us being alerted much earlier."

His lips thin, and he swivels right to clear the next hallway before answering. "I didn't think so before, but now…"

"Can we even trust the people currently inside this house?" I say with a growl and think of Olivia upstairs, alone with only a steel door to keep her safe.

"I guess we're going to find out," he says. "But don't think I'm not feeling your pain just because Justine's not here. I had to send Ethan and Aaron to pick her up."

Two of our newer members. Yeah, I'd be fucking nervous, too.

Maybe having Olivia locked upstairs isn't the worst thing.

"Down," Jaxon shouts, shoving at my back as a shot whistles past my head.

That was fucking close and has my heart pumping harder than it has in a long time, but it's not enough to stop me from laying on my side and finding my target.

Two men stand at the end of the next hallway. I can't even begin to guess how the fuck they got into this section of the house, but that's a problem for me to worry about later. After they're all dead.

I fire once, and so does Jaxon. In seconds, both intruders are down and Jaxon is helping me back to my feet.

"There's definitely a traitor in these walls," he says. "Or at least, there was."

The likelihood that whoever turned against us has already fled the compound to avoid getting caught in the crossfire is high, and I can tell that realization hasn't been far from Jaxon's mind. Especially when he pulls out his phone, and I see he's texting Justine. Hopefully sending a warning that won't potentially alert anyone she's with that we know.

More shots echo through the house and voices yell while the stomping of feet get closer. I look over at Jaxon, face grim. "We're not going to make it to the north end of the compound."

"No, I don't think we are," he replies, both of us confirming what the other already knows: we're not reaching the help that waits there. That is, if they're even still alive.

"Take cover," Jaxon warns as we each step behind opposite walls.

Gunfire continues to erupt through the house, but at least now, the sounds are all coming from the same direction.

I position myself better and swap mags to make sure I'm using a full one while I have the chance. Just as I've cocked the pistol, bullets begin to whiz toward us, grazing the walls and sending drywall through the air.

With my gun gripped tightly in my hand and my heart pounding with adrenaline, I begin to fire back. It's just me and Jaxon against a dozen men, armed to the teeth. Their eyes burn with an eagerness to see us fall, but that's not going to happen.

As much as I want to push forward, I know we can't lose our cover. There isn't anything else to shield even just one of us in the hallway the intruders are creeping down. For them, though, they don't seem to mind losing men as long as at least some of them get where they need to.

My gun doesn't stop firing, and all too soon I'm switching mags. I still have five more for this pistol and three for my backup nine-millimeter shoved into the holster above my boots. Even knowing that, I'm careful with each shot, not wanting one bullet to be wasted if I can help it.

Blood continues to shed around us, and more men fall, but more keep coming, like fucking roaches. The acrid scent of gunpowder fills the now-dim hallway, thanks to the lights being shot out at some point.

Even with all the chaos, time seems to slow down, and I can begin to see a pattern in how the intruders keep pushing forward. With that knowledge, I know I can't stand here behind the wall any longer. This needs to end now.

"I'm going in," I tell Jaxon above the cacophony of gunshots. "Watch my back."

"Always," he replies in confirmation, and I move out from behind the protection of the wall.

Shouts sound from the other men. I've ruined their plan by doing what they don't expect and charging forward. I use their confusion to my advantage and continue firing as I weave through the hail of bullets still coming my way.

My movements remain fluid and instinctual, and every squeeze of the trigger is accompanied by the satisfying thud of bodies hitting the ground, one after another.

Bullets continue to fly toward me, most of them sailing by, but it's not long before my left arm is grazed and my chest is hit. Thanks to the bulletproof vest, the shot only serves to take my breath away. Though, that doesn't stop my movements. Neither does my bleeding arm.

Our enemies don't seem to be as well-trained, but they're relentless. They continue to advance, their numbers seemingly endless even after the last dozen I've shot down since pushing forward. I grit my teeth, refusing to falter as Olivia's face flashes in my mind, fueling my determination.

Jaxon joins me, standing by my side when I wish he'd stayed behind the wall, but I can't be angry with his choice as we start to finally pull ahead, thinning their ranks with finally no new intruders joining them.

With only four men left to take down, I switch my mag one last time and pull the trigger just a few more times. But as I want to celebrate, pain sears through my right thigh, causing me to stumble forward, losing my footing.

"Fuck," I snarl, trying to get back up, but Jaxon warns me to stay down as he takes down two more men on his own.

One quick glance down at my leg tells me all I need to know: I'm completely fucked if another wave of men comes through here.

Blood seeps through my pants, dripping onto the already tattered floor. Jaxon has his shirt off before I can think what to do next and is securing it around the wound.

"That needs to stay tight," he warns. "If the bullet hit your femoral artery, having your house broken into is going to be the least of your worries before long."

I fucking wish he was wrong, but I know he's not. We've lost plenty of other men thanks to hits just like this one. If I have any intention of getting back to Olivia, I have to be smart with my next moves.

The pounding of more footsteps sounds behind us, and I twist with my gun pointed outward. Jaxon steps in front of me, doing the same, but it's Markus who comes around the corner, allowing me to breathe a little easier.

"Shit," he says, surveying the damages. "You two had the worst of it and the least help."

"Are they all dead?" I ask, not caring about anything else. If we're no longer under attack, I can release Olivia from the room and confirm she's okay.

Markus nods. "As far as I can tell. We lost at least half a dozen of our men with even more injured. How do we want to start the clean up and get everyone help?" He eyes my arm and leg closer. "Especially you."

I don't have time for this. At least I don't want to.

"Find Damon and follow whatever he says," I reply, then reach for Jaxon who carefully helps me stand on my one good leg. "Get me to the elevator."

I can tell Jaxon wants to argue and that Markus would prefer for me to get to a doctor first, but I'm not going anywhere else without Olivia.

28

OLIVIA

My knee can't stop bouncing, and I'm certain my heart is about to burst right out of my chest. Sitting here, staring at the door, and then glancing at my phone every minute is bound to be the death of me.

I'm supposed to be safe in the apartment, but that doesn't mean I can't hear all the gunfire below or that I'm not losing my fucking mind, having no clue if Luca and his men are winning or losing in whatever battle is happening just underneath me.

I want to call him or even Justine, but I'm afraid the moment I use my phone and allow myself to be distracted is the one that someone will break through that steel door, ready to kill me.

Minutes tick painfully by, and my palm grows sweaty from holding the borrowed pistol, but I don't release it. Not even when it begins to feel too heavy in my hands.

Today will not be my last day on this Earth. I'll make

fucking sure of that. My panic might be rising with the passing time, but so does my resolve.

This world, it's utterly fucked up, but I've only just found it, and after the last couple of days with Luca, I'm no longer prepared to let it go. I fully intend to fight for what I want, and I don't plan on losing.

Too much has already been taken from me. I refuse to let there be more. First, I lost my relationship with my father when he left, disappearing to wherever, then my teenage years from having to grow up so fast, and most recently my mother.

No longer will I be helpless. I can't accept that as my fate. Not when I know I deserve so much more.

Maybe not a life filled with murder and lingering threats, but maybe it doesn't always have to be this way. I won't know unless I stick around.

Luca has managed to build Monroe Investments, something that seems to be more than successful. He couldn't have done that if he was always on the hunt. At least, I hope not.

My fingers drum over my thigh as I try to relax for a second against the couch cushions, but the adrenaline caused by all the gunfire below won't allow that to happen.

Just when I consider closing my eyes in an attempt at centering myself, I hear the beep of numbers being pushed on the door.

Panic begins to claw its way up my throat, but then I remind myself that Luca wouldn't have given that code to anyone who couldn't be trusted. Anyone else would be trying to break it down, hopefully getting electrocuted in the process.

When the lock disengages and the handle begins to turn, I stand, remembering Tori's dad reiterating his instruction to me all those years ago.

Stand with your legs shoulder-length apart but have your right foot just a little more forward. Yes, Livie, just like that. Now, relax your arms as you raise them and only lock that right elbow enough to help absorb the impact when you pull the trigger. And don't forget to keep your wrists secure, or you'll risk jamming your firearm. You need the recoil to move through you, not to jolt your body.

If only I'd continued with my lessons as I got older, something I intend to do just as soon as this nightmare is over.

Using the memory to find a comfortable position, I keep my index finger hovering right over the trigger as the door opens slowly.

Nobody enters, but a voice I at least recognize sounds. "Olivia? Is it safe to come in?"

Like I would be able to say "no" if it wasn't. Seems like a rather stupid question. Still, I don't lower my guard.

"Yep. Where's Luca?" I ask cautiously, trying to not allow myself to think of all the reasons he wouldn't be here himself.

The man with the scar on his cheek peeks his head around the door and grins when he sees me standing there. "He got hurt, but he's okay. Just needs to see a doctor first. The worst of the trouble should be over for now, and he wants you to get out of here. Justine's waiting for you, too."

This is the same man who put his hands on my neck in the SUV that first night and also who I bumped into in the hallway only earlier today. So, it's not as if I don't know Luca considers him trustworthy enough to stay close, but still. Going with him gives me pause.

"How did Luca get hurt?" I ask, keeping my gun raised.

He proceeds further into the room but maintains a safe distance from me. "Not sure. I was fighting on the other side of the house. I can take you to the hospital instead of the safe house with Justine, but you'll have to keep that gun to my head, so Luca doesn't kill me himself for not doing as he demanded."

This has me smirking a little, because it's the kind of reaction I should know to expect from Luca by now.

"And Luca will be going to this safe house once he's been seen?" I ask, and he nods. "What's your name?" That might be helpful to know if I'm going to leave with him.

"Vin," he answers, remaining calm even though I'm still pointing a weapon at his head. "I've worked for the Monroe family for nearly twenty years now and if it makes you feel better, you can still point that gun at me all the way to the safe house. We just really need to get going."

I appraise him once more, taking in the blood splatter on his grey shirt and the gun at his hip that he hasn't once reached for. If he was a complete stranger, I don't think I would go with him, but given this is our third interaction and he doesn't mind me keeping the gun, I don't risk further upsetting Luca and at least lower my pistol.

Though, my eyes narrow on him as I do. "If you're lying, you should be aware that I'm not afraid to kill you."

He chuckles, the sound softening the hard lines of his face. "You wouldn't be Luca's woman if not. Now, let's get the fuck out of here."

He turns away from me, giving me his back, trusting me to follow and further easing my suspicions.

I grab my phone, shove it in my back pocket, then proceed to walk after Vin, still with the weapon in my hand, but resting at my side.

He's waiting at the wall on the left of the landing, a hidden panel opened and revealing a set of stairs. "We need to take these. The elevators are out from all the chaos."

Fucking stairs. Not what I want to do right now, but I follow him once more, jogging as quickly as I can without risking a fall. The last thing anyone needs is for me to kiss the concrete steps with my face.

By the time we reach the bottom, my legs are burning, but my lungs handle the exertion better than I expect. I guess I have Justine to thank for that when I see her since she's the one that got me into the gym that first time.

Vin opens a door, and on the other side is the familiarity of the garage that Luca has parked in both times I've been in the vehicle with him.

There's a waiting SUV just up ahead and more men

standing guard, and even though I don't recognize the others, that doesn't surprise me. It's not as if I've been paraded around the people who work for Luca over the last few weeks.

Vin is about ten feet ahead of me, and he opens the back passenger's door, gesturing with his hand for me to get in.

My chest twists with a tightness I don't like, but I consider the facts. Vin had the code, and he hasn't disarmed me. Someone trying to kidnap me probably wouldn't allow me to have a weapon.

With a slight shake of my head, I stop being so paranoid and step forward, but before I can get any further, a gunshot reverberates through the underground garage, hurting my ears and making me wince.

I start to duck, having no clue where it came from, just knowing that it's close. As I get to my knees, I see Vin's lifeless eyes staring at me and his body crumpled on the ground.

Mother fuck fuck.

There's no time to think. I merely push back up to my feet, turning to run in the opposite direction, only there's an imposing figure blocking my path. A behemoth of a man with a shaved head, dark eyes, and a smile that tells me I'm utterly fucked.

He rips the gun from my hand and shoves me backward. "Don't keep Titan waiting."

There's an accent lacing his curt words. Russian, maybe? German? Hell, I don't know at this point. My ears are ringing, and my entire body trembles as I attempt to stay upright.

Titan is here. The man who I've never even laid eyes on yet wants me dead because of something I saw. None of this feels real, but that doesn't mean I'm giving up.

My gaze moves left and right, and there are more men with more guns. There's literally nowhere else to go but closer to the dead body and waiting SUV. I could run, but something tells me I stand a better chance of getting out of this alive if I behave just a little longer.

Luca is going to be so fucking pissed.

The Russian continues to poke at my back, forcing me closer to the waiting open door. When I'm mere feet away, I avert my eyes while doing my best not to step on Vin's body. I'm still not certain he set me up from all earlier reasons and the fact that he's dead now, but a desire still builds within me to stomp my foot over his head for putting me in this position.

Once I'm at the open door and looking inside the dark interior, I have to blink several times for the image to make any sense to my overwhelmed brain. When it does, I still don't believe what I'm seeing. Titan is supposed to be here, but the man staring back at me...

All breath leaves my body, and I can't move. Shock has taken over, paralyzing me in this moment that makes absolutely no fucking sense.

The man I shouldn't recognize smiles at me, causing an unwelcome flutter to rise within my chest.

"Hello, Daughter," he says with a casual wave. "I

know it's been a while, but why don't you get in so we can have a little chat, yeah?"

Fuck my life.

———

Thank you for reading Ruthless Truths, Veiled Vengeance Book One!

That's one hell of an ending, but you can grab Tangled Deceit today on Amazon and Kindle Unlimited to complete the series.

After that, don't miss out on your chance to read the story short about Justine and Jaxon's beginning. Grab your FREE e-copy HERE. There is an option to sign up for my newsletter, but it's not required to read the story :)

STAY IN TOUCH

Find Heather on Facebook:

Reader Group

Want to talk all things books and get updates before anyone else? Come hang with me in my reader group/s:
Harper Reed's Romance Insiders (smutty contemporary stuff here)
Heather Renee's Book Warriors (mostly paranormal romance stuff here)

Author Page

Teaser and big updates are also posted here:
Harper Reed Books
Heather Renee Author

ALSO BY THE AUTHORS

Contemporary Romance books as Harper Reed:

The Unexpected Series

A Spicy RomCom trilogy featuring three best friends and their happily-ever-afters!

A Mutually Beneficial Proposal

A Mutually Beneficial Mistake

A Mutually Beneficial Secret

Standalones

A Royal Oops

A Spicy RomCom with royal antics, an epic second chance romance, and a kingdom that needs their new queen.

Paranormal Romance books as Heather Renee:

Mystics and Mayhem World—Series are connected by characters crossovers, but not the plots. You can read them in any order.

Broken Court

A complete New Adult Urban Fantasy series featuring an unconventional and anti-heroine leading lady, a broody love interest, and a fae kingdom with a vile king.

Luna Marked

A complete New Adult wolf shifter series (dual POV) featuring a strong-willed leading lady and a patient, yet fierce alpha male.

Scorned by Blood

A complete New Adult Vampire series featuring a supernatural hunter and the sexy vampire bound to protect her no matter the cost.

Fated to the Wolf

A complete New Adult Witch and Wolf series (dual POV) featuring an abandoned witch, a rogue wolf, and their broken bond.

The Hidden Realm

A complete New Adult wolf and dragon shifter series (dual POV) featuring a feisty wolf shifter just looking for her freedom and a broody dragon trying to save his world.

Individual Series

Raven Point Pack Series

A complete Upper Young Adult Paranormal Romance series featuring wolves, witches, vengeance, and fated mates.

Shadow Veil Academy

A complete Upper Young Adult Urban Fantasy Academy series featuring shifters, elves, witches, and more.

Elite Supernatural Trackers

A complete New Adult Urban Fantasy series featuring witches, demons, a smart-mouthed female lead, alpha males, and a snarky fairy sidekick.

Royal Fae Guardians

A complete Young Adult Urban Fantasy series featuring fae, magic users, a sweet romance, along with snark and humor.

Blood of the Sea Series

A complete Young Adult Paranormal Romance series featuring vampires, open seas adventures, and the occasional pirate.

Standalone Books

Ignite Me - A spicy wolf shifter story featuring a lost heir, the mate who doesn't want her, and the enemies who wish them dead.

Marked Paradox - A Young Adult fae story about a realm divided and one fae to bring them back together.

ABOUT THE AUTHORS

Heather Renee and Harper Reed are actually one in the same. Under Heather Renee, I write slow burn Paranormal Romance and with Harper Reed I get to let loose with steamier contemporary romance. The second name is just so readers can easily identify the varying genres.

My love of reading eventually led to the passion of writing and giving the gift of escapism. When I'm not chatting with the voices in my head, you can usually find me spending time with my family, going on our own adventures, or curled up on the couch with a good book!

If you want to learn more about my books or hang out with me on social media, you can find me in the following places:

For Heather Renee

Newsletter—Reader Group—Facebook Page—Instagram—TikTok—Website—Amazon—Bookbub

For Harper Reed

Reader Group—Facebook Page—Instagram—TikTok—Website—Amazon—Bookbub